THE WIZARD OF OZ

THE SCREENPLAY

WITHDRAWN

THE WIZARD OF OZ

Noel Langley
Florence Ryerson
and Edgar Allan Woolf

From the book by

L. FRANK BAUM

Edited by
Michael Patrick Hearn

faber and faber

First published in 1989
by Dell Publishing
a division of
Bantam Doubleday Dell Publishing Group, Inc
Screenplay first published in 1991
by Faber and Faber Limited
3 Queen Square London WC1N 3AU

This edition in 2001
Typeset by RefineCatch Limited, Bungay, Suffolk
Printed in England by Mackays of Chatham plc

Grateful acknowledgement is made for permission to reprint the following:
'If I were King of the Forest' by E. Y. Harburg and Harold Arlen. Copyright © 1938
(Renewed 1966) Metro-Goldwyn-Mayer, Inc. Rights Assigned to SBK Catalogue
Partnership. All Rights Controlled and Administered by SBK Feist Catalog, Inc. All
Rights Reserved. International Copyright Secured. Used by Permission.

'If I only had a Brain, (If I only had a Heart), (If I only had the Nerve)'; 'Ding Dong!
The Witch is Dead'; 'Merry Old Land of Oz' and 'The Jitterbug' by E. Y. Harburg and
Harold Arlen. Copyright © 1938, 1939 (Renewed 1966, 1967) Metro-Goldwyn-Mayer,
Inc. Rights Assigned to SBK Catalogue Partnership. All Rights Controlled
and Administered by SBK Feist Catalog, Inc. All Rights Reserved. International
Copyright Secured. Used by Permission.

'Over the Rainbow' by E. Y. Harburg and Harold Arlen. Copyright © 1938, 1939
(Renewed 1966, 1967) Metro-Goldwyn-Mayer, Inc. Assigned to Leo Feist, Inc. Rights of
Leo Feist, Inc. Assigned to SBK Catalogue Partnership. All Rights Controlled and
Administered by SBK Feist Catalog, Inc. International Copyright Secured. Made in USA.
Used by Permission.

'We're off to See the Wizard' by E. Y. Harburg and Harold Arlen. Copyright © 1938,
1939 (Renewed 1966, 1967) Metro-Goldwyn-Mayer, Inc. Rights Assigned to SBK
Catalogue Partnership. All Rights throughout the world Controlled and Administered
by SBK Feist Catalog, Inc. International Copyright Secured. Made in USA.
All Rights Reserved.

A CIP record for this book is available from the British Library

ISBN 0-571-21093-7

2 4 6 8 10 9 7 5 3 1

CONTENTS

THE WIZARD OF OZ

THE SCREENPLAY

FADE IN

For nearly forty years this story has given faithful service to the Young in Heart; and Time has been powerless to put its kindly philosophy out of fashion.

To those of you who have been faithful to it in return

. . . and to the Young in Heart – we dedicate this picture.

FADE OUT

FADE IN
LONG SHOT – COUNTRY ROAD – DAY

From the foreground a long straight road leads to and past the farm. Into the shot, from past Camera, half running and half walking backward, comes Dorothy, a little girl of twelve, and her dog, Toto. She stops a moment, and looks down the road in the direction from which she came. She seems a little breathless and apprehensive.

MEDIUM SHOT – DOROTHY

Dorothy (*to Toto*) She isn't coming yet, Toto . . .
(*kneeling down and examining him*)
Did she hurt you? She tried to, didn't she?
(*rising as she picks up books and starts along road toward home*)
Come on – we'll go tell Uncle Henry and Auntie Em . . .
Come on, Toto!

LONG SHOT – GALE FARM – PORCH AND SIDE YARD

Dorothy comes running in the gate from the road and around to the side of the house where Aunt Em and Uncle Henry are working with an old coal-oil five-hundred-chick incubator.

Dorothy (*as she runs*) Aunt – Em –! Aunt – Em –!

THREE SHOT – AUNT EM, UNCLE HENRY, AND DOROTHY

Uncle Henry and Aunt Em with worried faces are taking small live chicks from the incubator, putting them quickly under clucking, broody hens, which are nearby in crates. They count to themselves as Dorothy runs into scene. Aunt Em wears a cooking apron.

Dorothy Aunt – Em –!

Aunt Em (*putting live chicks into her apron*) Sixty-seven, sixty-eight –

Dorothy (*breathless*) Just listen to what Miss Gulch did to Toto! She –

Aunt Em Dorothy – *please* – we're trying to count! Sixty-eight . . .

Dorothy Oh, but Aunt Em, she hit him over the –

Uncle Henry Don't bother us now, honey. This old incubator's gone bad, and we're likely to lose a lot of our chicks.

Dorothy (*picking up a chick*) Oh – oh, the poor little things . . .
(*then back to the subject of Toto again*)
Oh, but Aunt Em – Miss Gulch hit Toto right over the back with a rake – just because she says he gets in her garden and chases her nasty old cat every day!

Aunt Em (*taking Dorothy's chick to put under a hen*)
Seventy –
(*then more exasperated*)
Dorothy, *please*!

Dorothy Oh, but he doesn't do it every day – just once or twice a week – and he can't catch her old cat anyway. And now she says she's going to get the Sheriff – and –

Aunt Em Dorothy, Dorothy – *we're busy*!

Dorothy (*mournfully*) Oh, all right.
(*She walks offscreen, toward the barnyard.*)

MEDIUM SHOT – BACK OF HOUSE – BARNYARD

Zeke, Hunk, and Hickory, farm hands, are busy straining to lift the body of a large wagon onto the wheels. It has been patched up with old boards, etc. Dorothy enters the scene.

Zeke How's she coming?

Hunk Take it easy. Ow! – you got my finger!

Zeke Well, why don't you get your finger out of the way?

Hickory There you are.

Hunk Right on my finger!

Zeke It's a lucky thing it wasn't your head.

Dorothy Zeke, what am I going to do about Miss Gulch? Just because Toto chases her old cat –

Zeke (*hurrying away*) Listen, honey – I got them hogs to get in.

He hurries away, followed by Hickory. Hunk takes up a hammer to drive in a bolt.

Hunk Now lookit, Dorothy – you ain't using your head

5

about Miss Gulch. Think you didn't have any brains at all!

Dorothy I have *so* got brains!

Hunk Well, why don't you use 'em! When you come home, don't go by Miss Gulch's place. Then Toto won't get in her garden, and you won't get in no trouble, see?

Dorothy (*knowing he's right but not willing to admit it because of his patronizing attitude*) Oh, Hunk – you just won't listen, that's all.
(*She goes away toward Zeke offscreen.*)

Hunk (*calling after her as he hammers*) Well, your head ain't made of straw, you know!
(*On this, not looking at what he is doing, he hammers his injured finger again.*)
Ow! (*whirling around*)

LONG SHOT – ZEKE AT STY GATE

He is calling hogs as they come in past Camera from the yard. In the background Dorothy approaches him from behind and climbs up on the fence, walking on it and balancing herself.

Zeke Soo-eee! (*shooing in a wayward hog*) Get in there before I make a dime bank outa ya! (*pouring feed in trough*) Listen, kid – are you going to let that old Gulch heifer try and buffalo ya? She ain't nothing to be afraid of. Have a little courage, that's all.

Dorothy I'm not afraid of her.

Zeke Then the next time she squawks, walk right up to her and spit in her eye. That's what I'd do.

Dorothy (*tottering with a scream*) Oh!
(*She falls into pen.*)

Oh! Oh, Zeke! Help! Help me, Zeke, get me out of here!
Help! Oh! Oh!

*Zeke is over the fence like lightning, takes Dorothy's
foot out of a wire, and carries her out over the pen. He
jumps out as Hickory and Hunk come running, sits
down, and begins wiping his brow.*

Hickory Are you all right, Dorothy?

Dorothy (*shaken*) Yes, I'm all right. Oh, I fell in and – and
Zeke –
(*Looking at Zeke, who is shaking and wiping his head
with his handkerchief – she laughs.*)
Why, Zeke – you're just as scared as I am!

Hunk (*laughing at Zeke with Hickory*) What's the matter?
Gonna let a little old pig make a coward out of ya?

Hickory Look at you, Zeke – you're just as white –

*At this point, Aunt Em comes up carrying a bowl of
crullers.*

Aunt Em Here – here – what's all this jabber-wapping
when there's work to be done! I know three shiftless
farm hands that'll be out of a job before they know it.

Hickory (*trying to explain*) Well, Dorothy was walking
along –

Aunt Em I saw you tinkering with that contraption,
Hickory! Now you and Hunk get back to that wagon.

Hickory (*shaking his finger in the air*) All right, Mrs
Gale – but someday they're going to erect a statue to me
in this town, and –

Aunt Em Well, don't start posing for it now!

Hunk laughs at him.

7

Here – here – can't work on an empty stomach. Have some crullers.
(*She passes them around.*)

Hunk Gosh, Mrs Gale!

Hickory (*taking some*) Oh, thanks.

Aunt Em Just fried.

Hunk Swell!

Hickory and Hunk dart off.

Zeke (*trying to explain, as he takes a cruller*) You see – Dorothy toppled in with the big Duroc –

Aunt Em It's no place for Dorothy around a pigsty! Now, you go feed those hogs before they worry themselves into anemia!

Zeke (*exiting*) Yes'm.

Aunt Em starts back toward the house, as Dorothy takes a cruller and follows her. We truck with them.

Dorothy Auntie Em – really – you know what Miss Gulch said she was going to do to Toto? She said she was gonna –

Aunt Em Now, Dorothy dear – stop imagining things . . . you always get yourself into a fret over nothing.

Dorothy No –

Aunt Em Now, you just help us out today and find yourself a place where you won't get into any trouble!

Aunt Em goes on as we hold and Dorothy stands looking sadly after her, munching her cruller. She looks down at Toto.

Dorothy Someplace where there isn't any trouble . . .
(*tossing a piece to Toto*)

... do you suppose there is such a place, Toto?
(*dreamily to herself*)
There must be. It's not a place you can get to by a boat or
a train.
It's far, far away ...
(*Music starts.*)
Behind the moon.
Beyond the rain.
(*singing*)
Somewhere, over the rainbow, way up high,
There's a land that I heard of once in a lullaby.

Somewhere, over the rainbow, skies are blue,
And the dreams that you dare to dream really do come
    true.

Someday I'll wish upon a star
And wake up where the clouds are far behind me,
Where troubles melt like lemon drops,

Away above the chimney tops
That's where you'll find me.

Somewhere over the rainbow, bluebirds fly,
Birds fly over the rainbow,
Why then, oh why can't I?

SHOT OF SUN RAYS THROUGH CLOUDS

Dorothy (*singing*)
    If happy little bluebirds fly
    Beyond the rainbow,
    Why oh why can't I?

LONG SHOT – THE ROADWAY – APPROACHING
THE FARM

*This is a narrow little lane. A bicycle is pedaling along
with Miss Gulch sitting stiffly on the seat. There is a*

basket strapped to the back of the cycle. A rolled
umbrella is fastened to the handlebar.

The Camera follows her as she reaches the gate to the
farmhouse. Uncle Henry is painting the fence.

Miss Gulch (*as she gets off bicycle and takes basket from
rear*) Mr Gale!

Uncle Henry (*without any enthusiasm, as he opens the
swinging gate for her*) Howdy, Miss Gulch.

Miss Gulch (*sharply*) I want to see you and your wife right
away about Dorothy.

Uncle Henry (*worried*) Dorothy? Well, what has Dorothy
done?

Miss Gulch (*indignantly*) What's she done? I'm all but
lame from the bite on my leg!

Uncle Henry You mean she bit ya?

Miss Gulch No, her dog!

Uncle Henry Oh, she bit her dog, eh?

He drops his hold on the gate, which swings closed and
gives Miss Gulch a smart little spank.

Miss Gulch (*after the gate hits her*) No!

LAP DISSOLVE TO:
INT. GALE SITTING ROOM

It is a typical old-fashioned farmhouse parlor. Flowered
wallpaper, family pictures on the wall, plush furniture,
etc.

Aunt Em and Miss Gulch are seated as Dorothy enters
with Toto in her arms. In the background Uncle Henry is
looking very unhappy.

Miss Gulch (*to Aunt Em*) That dog's a menace to the community. I'm taking him to the Sheriff and make sure he's destroyed.

Dorothy Destroyed? Toto? Oh, you can't . . . you mustn't . . . Auntie Em – Uncle Henry – you won't let her . . . will you?

Uncle Henry Uh . . . ah . . . course, we won't . . . eh . . . a . . .
(*his voice breaking a little, uncertain, as he looks at his wife*)
Will we, Em?

Dorothy Please, Aunt Em! Toto didn't mean to. He didn't know he was doing anything wrong. I'm the one that ought to be punished. I let him go in her garden . . . you can send me to bed without supper –

Miss Gulch (*angrily, to Aunt Em*) If you don't hand over that dog, I'll bring a damage suit that'll take your whole farm! There's a law protectin' folks against dogs that bite!

Aunt Em (*to Miss Gulch, dryly*) How would it be if she keeps him tied up? He's really gentle – with gentle people, that is.

Miss Gulch Well, that's for the Sheriff to decide –
(*producing a paper for Aunt Em*)
– here's his order allowing me to take him –
(*warningly*)
– unless you want to go against the law.

Uncle Henry (*looking at order*) Uh – yeah –

Aunt Em We can't go against the law, Dorothy.
(*It is plain that she is struggling to hide some emotion.*)
I'm afraid poor Toto will have to go.

Miss Gulch Now you're seeing reason.

Dorothy No –

Miss Gulch (*producing basket*) Here's what I'm taking him in so he can't attack me again!

Dorothy (*going suddenly berserk as she sees Miss Gulch coming toward her*) Oh, no – no – I won't let you take him. You go away you – ooh – I'll bite you myself!

Aunt Em Dorothy!

Dorothy (*wildly*) You wicked old witch! Uncle Henry, Auntie Em! Don't let 'em take Toto! Don't let her take him – please!

Miss Gulch I've got a notice! Let me have him!

Dorothy Stop her!

Aunt Em (*almost unable to speak*) Put him in the basket, Henry.

Henry, very reluctantly, puts Toto in the basket Miss Gulch is holding.

Miss Gulch The idea!

Dorothy Oh, don't, Uncle Henry. Oh, Toto! Don't . . .

With an expression of utter despair, she runs out of the room, sobbing. Aunt Em stands looking at Miss Gulch with an expression of repressed anger.

Aunt Em Almira Gulch . . . just because you own half the county doesn't mean you have the power to run the rest of us! For twenty-three years I've been dying to tell you what I thought of you . . . and now . . . well – being a Christian woman – I can't say it!

She, too, runs off as Uncle Henry sits down, chuckling, with Miss Gulch aghast at what she has heard.

DISSOLVE TO:
EXT. ROADWAY – CLOSE ON MISS GULCH

> Miss Gulch is pedaling along, the basket strapped to the rear of the bicycle. The lid is bumping up and down, straining the catch.
>
> Toto manages to work the catch loose. He scrambles out of the basket. The Camera pans to show him streaking back toward the farm.

QUICK LAP TO:
INT. DOROTHY'S ROOM

> On the night table is a picture of Dorothy and Aunt Em standing at the farm gate.
>
> Dorothy is sitting on the floor by Toto's bed, still crying. Toto barks as he hurtles through the open window in one wild leap and lands on the bed.

Dorothy Toto! Darling! Oh, I got you back! You came back! Oh, I'm so glad! Toto!
(*She hugs him happily for a moment, then suddenly realizes their danger.*)
Oh, they'll be coming back for you in a minute. We've got to get away!
(*She holds him close and then pulls an ancient straw bag out from under the bed.*)
We've got to run away!

LAP DISSOLVE TO:
EXTREME CLOSE ON A DUSTY ROAD

> This is shooting straight down and gets two rows of rather pathetic little footprints . . . one set made by Dorothy, one by Toto. The soundtrack carries music that suggests weariness. Move Camera along to get the feet that are making the prints.

Dorothy is going down the road with her bag and basket. Toto is trotting a bit to one side. The two look very small and forlorn against the immensity of the prairie, which spreads out in every direction.

LAP DISSOLVE TO:
LONG SHOT – BRIDGE AND GULLY

The same figures are just passing across a bridge. In the foreground is a little gully. Beside it is a decorated wagon – all very dusty and shabby. Humming of a voice comes over scene as Dorothy reads the large lettering on the wagon:

PROFESSOR

MARVEL

ACCLAIMED BY

The CROWNED HEADS of EUROPE

LET HIM   IN HIS
    READ YOUR PAST PRESENT and FUTURE   CRYSTAL
        ALSO JUGGLING AND SLEIGHT OF HAND

To the side of the entrance reads: BALLOON EXHIBITIONIST. *The humming voice is coming from a man we shall know as Professor Marvel, an old carnival fakir, who steps down out of the wagon and walks over to the fire.*

Professor Marvel Well – well – well! Houseguests, huh? Ha, ha, ha, ha! And who might you be? Heh!
(*before Dorothy starts to answer*)
No, no, no, now don't tell me!
(*He puts his hand to his brow like a mind reader. When he speaks, it is in the typical patter of a sideshow fakir. He sits down and picks up toasting fork.*)
Let's see . . . you're . . . you're traveling in disguise – No! that's not right . . . I . . . you're . . . you're going on a visit – No! I'm wrong . . . that's . . . you're . . . you're . . . *running away!*

Dorothy How did you guess?

Professor Marvel Ha, ha! Professor Marvel never guesses – he *knows*! Heh, heh! Now *why* are you running away?

Dorothy Why . . .

Professor Marvel No, no, now don't tell me. They . . . they don't understand you at home. They don't appreciate you . . . you want to see other lands – big cities – big mountains – big oceans . . . heh!

Dorothy (*in awed tones*) Why, it's just like you could read what was inside of me.

Professor Marvel (*laughs*) Ye-heh –

Toto runs forward and grabs a wienie off the Professor's fork.

Dorothy Oh, Toto! That's not polite! We haven't been asked yet!

Professor Marvel Ha, ha, ha! He's perfectly welcome! Heh, heh! As one dog to another, huh?
(*Puts another wienie on the fork.*)
Ha, ha, ha, ha! Here now . . . let's see . . . where were we?

Dorothy (*remembering the sign*) Oh, please, Professor, why can't we go with you and see all the crowned heads of Europe?

Professor Marvel Do you know any? (*suddenly remembering the sign*) Oh, you mean the thing, yes . . . Well, I . . . I never do anything without consulting my crystal first. (*rising*) Let's go inside here. We'll . . . just come along. I'll show you . . .
(*He leads her into the wagon.*)

INT. WAGON

Dorothy and the Professor enter. The wagon is fitted up with the usual hocus-pocus, such as a fortune-telling booth. The Professor seats Dorothy as he dons a headdress and lights two candles on both sides of his chair and sits opposite her.

Professor Marvel That's right. Here, sit right down here. That's it. Heh, heh! (*indicating crystal*) This . . . this is the same, genuine, magic, authentic crystal used by the priests of Isis and Osiris in the days of the Pharaohs of Egypt . . . in which Cleopatra first saw the approach of Julius Caesar and Marc Antony . . . and . . . and so on and so on. Now, eh, you ah . . . you'd better close your eyes, my child, for a moment . . . in order to be better in tune with the infinite . . .

Dorothy closes her eyes and he rummages through her basket.

. . . we . . . we can't do these things without reaching out into the infinite . . .
(*He flips out a photograph from the basket.*)

INSERT – A PHOTOGRAPH IN THE PROFESSOR'S HAND

This is the picture of the farm, with Dorothy and Aunt Em at the gate, which we saw earlier on Dorothy's table.

BACK TO SCENE

The Professor, evidently having gotten the cue he is looking for, puts the photograph under his leg and brings his patter to a quick close and gets down to business.

Professor Marvel Yes, that's . . . that's all right. Now you can open them. We'll gaze into the crystal! (*gazing into it*) Ah, what's this I see? A house . . . with a picket fence and a barn with a weather vane and . . . of a . . . of a . . . running horse.

Dorothy That's our farm!

Professor Marvel (*laughs*) Yes . . . yes . . . there's . . .

there's . . . a woman . . . she's . . . she's wearing a . . . a . . . polka-dot dress . . . her face is care-worn . . .

Dorothy That's Aunt Em!

Professor Marvel (*as if reminded*) Yes, her . . . her name is Emily.

Dorothy (*eagerly*) That's right. What's she doing?

Professor Marvel Well . . . I . . . I can't quite see . . . Why – she's crying!

Dorothy Oh!

Professor Marvel Someone has hurt her . . . someone has just about broken her heart . . .

Dorothy (*in a small, guilty voice*) Me?

Professor Marvel Well, it's . . . it's someone she loves very much. Someone she's been very kind to. Someone she's taken care of in sickness.

Dorothy (*beginning to be affected*) I had the measles once . . . and she stayed right by me every minute!

Professor Marvel Uh-huh.

Dorothy What's she doing now?

Professor Marvel (*dramatically*) Eh, she's . . . (*gazing into the crystal*) . . . what's this? Why, she's . . . she's putting her hand on her heart!

Dorothy gasps.

Why, she's . . . she's dropping down on the bed!

Dorothy (*distractedly*) Oh, no! No!

Professor Marvel Eh, that's all. The crystal's gone dark.

Dorothy (*rising*) Oh, you . . . you don't suppose she could really be sick, do you? Oh!

17

Professor Marvel Oh, well, I . . .

Dorothy Oh, I've got to go home right away!

Professor Marvel But what's this? I thought you were going along with me!

Dorothy (*picking up her basket*) Oh, no! No, I have to get to her right away! Come on, Toto! Come on!

Professor Marvel (*rising with photo in hand*) Huh?

LONG SHOT – REAR OF WAGON

Dorothy (*as she comes scrambling down the steps, picking up suitcase and Toto*) Come on! Good-bye, Professor Marvel, and thanks a lot!
(*She drops Toto, and they run out of scene.*)

LONG SHOT – PROFESSOR MARVEL

A gust of wind strikes the wagon and tosses the trees about, bringing down twigs and leaves. He glances up, concerned, and goes to his horse.

Professor Marvel (*to his horse*) Better get under cover, Sylvester! There's a storm blowin' up – a whopper, to speak in the vernacular of the peasantry.
(*worried, as he gazes after Dorothy*) Poor little kid! I hope she gets home all right.

LAP DISSOLVE TO:
LONG SHOT – GALE FARM

By now the sky is dark and ominous. The wind is whistling. A cyclone is approaching.

LONG SHOT – BARNYARD

Chickens are running. The wind is blowing weeds and dust.

Uncle Henry (*running in with Hunk*) Hunk, get them horses loose! Where's Hickory? Hickory! Hickory! Doggone it! Hick –

Zeke comes running in from outside.

Zeke (*terrified, looking up and out at the sky, pointing*) It's a twister . . . it's a twister!

The wind grows stronger. The horses run loose from the barn.

LONG SHOT – FARM

The cyclone is approaching.

EXT. FARMHOUSE – BY KITCHEN DOOR

Aunt Em (*wildly*) Dorothy! Dorothy!

LONG SHOT – ROADWAY

Dorothy and Toto struggle against the wind. The cyclone is behind them.

LONG SHOT – BARNYARD

Uncle Henry and the farm hands turn a horse loose, and they run after it.

Uncle Henry Come on! Everybody in the storm cellar!

ROADWAY – ANOTHER SHOT OF DOROTHY AND TOTO

Weeds and branches are blowing by them. She picks up Toto.

LONG SHOT – STORM CELLAR

Everyone rushing to the storm cellar.

Aunt Em Henry! Henry! I can't find Dorothy! She's somewhere out in the storm! Dorothy!

Uncle Henry Gosh, we can't look for her now!

Aunt Em Dorothy!

Uncle Henry Come on! Get in the cellar! Hurry up!

They start to go down into the cellar.

LONG SHOT – GALE FARM

Dorothy reaches the gate. Camera pans as she comes to the house. When she opens the screen door, it flies off in the wind. She goes inside.

LONG SHOT – STORM CELLAR

Zeke and Hunk are now exiting down into the cellar and pulling the door shut after them.

INT. FARMHOUSE

Dorothy, carrying Toto, hurries from room to room.

During all of this the sound of the wind has been increasing until it is almost unbearable.

Dorothy (*wildly*) Auntie Em! Auntie Em! Auntie Em!

LONG SHOT – STORM CELLAR

Dorothy runs to the cellar door and tries to open it, but it will not budge. She then stamps on it with her foot.

Dorothy Auntie Em! Uncle Henry!
(*She rushes back into the house.*)

INT. DOROTHY'S BEDROOM

Dorothy looks out of the window and turns back.

Dorothy (*almost lost in the uproar*) Auntie Em! Oh!

As the blast hits the house, the window blows in and strikes her on the back of the head. She falls over onto her bed.

MONTAGE – CLOSE-UP – PRISM SHOT OF DOROTHY

Superimposed over shots of the whirling cyclone and the house whirling through space. These effects suggest the sensations of a person going under gas or ether.

This is the first scene of Dorothy's delirium. Up to now, nothing is shown that hasn't actually happened in real life. This, therefore, is the first scene of the fantasy.

MEDIUM SHOT – BEDROOM

Dorothy is beginning to pull herself up from the bed. She peers fearfully out of the window and sees the wreckage floating past: a chicken roost, a fence, a house, a buggy, a tree, a henhouse with a crowing rooster.

An Old Lady in a rocking chair sails past. She is knitting busily and rocking, seemingly unaware that she is no longer on her front porch. The Old Lady waves as she floats out of sight, and a cow sails past that moos at Dorothy mournfully. Toto barks.

A crate of fowl goes gently past. A small rowboat goes by, two men rowing furiously at the oars. They tip their hats and drift out of sight.

MEDIUM SHOT – DOROTHY

She peers down at the swirling funnel of the cyclone.

Dorothy (*shouting*) We must be up inside the cyclone!

CLOSE SHOT – TOTO

He peers out from under the bed.

MEDIUM SHOT – BEDROOM

Dorothy sees Miss Gulch pedaling away grimly on her bicycle.

Dorothy Oh, Miss Gulch!

When Miss Gulch comes close to the Camera, her clothes change into a flying robe and pointed hat of a witch, and her bicycle fades into a broom. She gives a wild, weird peal of laughter.

LONG SHOT – CYCLONE

The house spins up in the swirling funnel of the cyclone and then parts company with it.

LONG SHOT – DOROTHY

She screams as the bed spins and rolls around the floor.

LONG SHOT – PROCESS

The house begins to fall.

The house comes spiraling down through the air toward Camera, which is tilted up toward it. Eventually it hits Camera and blocks out the screen.

MEDIUM SHOT – DOROTHY AND TOTO

The house comes to a crashing halt.

Dorothy Oh!

There is dead silence on the soundtrack as Dorothy gets off the bed with Toto in her arms and picks up her basket and tiptoes to the door.

WIPE TO:
MEDIUM SHOT – INT. FRONT DOOR

As Dorothy opens the door slowly and peers out, a blaze of color greets her. This is the first time we see Technicolor. The Kansas scenes were all sepia washes. The inside of the door is monochrome, to give more contrast. When the door is open, the country is shown – a picture of bright greens and blues.

As Dorothy goes through the door, the Camera trucks after her and then, over her shoulder, to a full shot of the Munchkin Country. It is composed of sweeping hills and valleys and dips and waves in the ground; the grass is spangled with daisies; flowers grow everywhere, three or four times life-size, so that hollyhocks stand several feet in the air. The sky is bright blue with little white clouds; and a little stream runs near with huge lily pads on it.

Feeding the stream is an exquisite fountain. Surrounding the fountain are three or four steps, and to the back of it is Munchkinland's Civic Center, a quaint little piece of architecture. This is all close to the house in which Dorothy fell from Kansas.

The scene is quite empty of all signs of life, except the twittering of a bird or two in the distance.

LONG SHOT – DOROTHY

Toto is in her arms. We get the faintly underscored strains of 'Ding Dong! The Witch Is Dead!' The girl is looking around with an expression of delighted amazement.

Dorothy Toto, I've a feeling we're not in Kansas anymore . . .

To the strains of 'Over the Rainbow', Dorothy walks

*with Toto in her arms. Some Munchkin heads peer up
above the bushes and then vanish again.*

We must be over the rainbow!

LONG SHOT – THE COUNTRYSIDE

*Suddenly a large, pink-tinted crystal bubble, gleaming
like a soap bubble, approaches, getting bigger and bigger.
Dorothy steps aside as it bounces gently in the air before
her for a moment and then fades when it lands. The
Witch of the North dissolves in.*

CLOSE-UP – DOROTHY

At the sight of the Witch, she is astounded.

Dorothy (*to Toto*) Now I – I *know* we're not in Kansas.

LONGER ON SCENE

*Glinda comes gracefully forward. She chatters very
brightly and quickly and puts in a high trill of a giggle
wherever she can find room for it.*

Glinda Are you a good witch – or a bad witch?

*Dorothy is so sure Glinda can't be addressing her that
she looks around behind her. But there is nobody there.*

Dorothy (*turning back*) Who, me? Why – I'm not a witch
at all. I'm Dorothy Gale from Kansas.

Glinda (*pointing to Toto*) Oh, well, is *that* the witch?

CLOSE ON TOTO

GROUP SHOT – DOROTHY, WITCH, TOTO

Dorothy Who, Toto? Toto's my dog!

Glinda (*puzzled*) Well, I'm a little muddled – the
Munchkins called me because a new witch has just

dropped a house on the Wicked Witch of the East – and there's the house – and here *you* are – and that's all that's left of the Wicked Witch of the East.

Glinda points, and we cut in a quick close-up of two ruby slippers sticking out from under the house.

Dorothy Oh!

Glinda And so, what the Munchkins want to know is: Are you a good witch or a bad witch?

Dorothy Oh, but I've already told you, I'm not a witch at all – witches are old and ugly.

There is a musical peal of laughter from behind the bushes and flowers. Dorothy starts and looks about.

What was that?

Glinda (*smiling*) The Munchkins. They're laughing because I *am* a witch. I'm Glinda, the Witch of the North.

Dorothy You *are*? (*curtsies*) Oh, I beg your pardon! But I've never heard of a beautiful witch before!

Glinda Only bad witches are ugly. The Munchkins are happy because you have freed them from the Wicked Witch of the East.

Dorothy (*puzzled*) Oh, but if you please, what are Munchkins?

The musical laughter comes again from the Munchkins.

Glinda The little people who live in this land – it's Munchkinland . . . and you are their national heroine, my dear.
(*Glinda calls to the Munchkins.*)
It's all right – you may all come out and thank her!

(*singing*)
Come out, come out wherever you are.
And meet the young lady who fell from a star.

One by one the Munchkins get up courage to tiptoe out to music.

(*singing*)
She fell from the sky, she fell very far.
And Kansas she says is the name of the star.

Munchkins (*singing*)
Kansas she says is the name of the star.

By now the Munchkins are around Dorothy. They are quaint, jolly-looking little men and women.

Glinda (*singing*)
She brings you good news. Or haven't you heard?
When she fell out of Kansas, a miracle occurred.

Dorothy It really was no miracle. What happened was just this:
(*singing; modestly explaining to the Munchkins*)
The wind began to switch,
The house to pitch,
And suddenly the hinges started to unhitch.
Just then the witch
To satisfy an itch
Went flying on her broomstick thumbing for a hitch.

Munchkin (*a braggart*)
And oh what happened then was rich.

Several Munchkins
The house began to pitch,
The kitchen took a slitch.

All of the Munchkins
It landed on the Wicked Witch in the middle of a ditch

Which
Was not a healthy sitch-
Uation for
The Wicked Witch.
(*dancing*)
The house began to pitch,
The kitchen took a slitch.
It landed on the Wicked Witch in the middle of a ditch
Which
Was not a healthy sitch-
Uation for
The Wicked Witch
Who
Began to twitch
And was reduced
To just a stitch
Of what was once the Wicked Witch. (*cheering*)

A carriage drawn by ponies has driven up, and Dorothy steps in.

Munchkin No. 1
We thank you very sweetly
For doing it so neatly.

Munchkin No. 2
You've killed her so completely
That we thank you very sweetly.
(*handing her a bouquet*)

Glinda
Let the joyous news be spread
The wicked old witch at last is dead!

Camera booms as carriage moves forward, followed by a procession of Munchkin Soldiers.

All Munchkins (*with great gusto*)
Ding Dong, the witch is dead
Which old witch?

The wicked witch
Ding Dong, the wicked witch is dead!
Wake up, you sleepy head,
Rub your eyes,
Get out of bed.
Wake up, the wicked witch is dead!
She's gone where the goblins go
Below, below, below,
Yo ho let's open up and sing,
And ring the bells out:
Ding Dong! the merry-o
Sing it high,
Sing it low,
Let them know
The wicked witch is dead!

The carriage has stopped at the steps of Munchkinland's Civic Center. Fanfare . . . and three Heralds. Enter Mayor, who helps Dorothy out of the carriage and takes her up the steps to six City Fathers, Barrister, etc.

Mayor (*singing*)
As Mayor of the Munchkin City
In the County of the Land of Oz,
I welcome you most regally.

Barrister (*singing*)
But we've got to verify it legally.
To see . . .

Mayor
To see . . .

Barrister
If she . . .

Mayor
If she . . .

28

Barrister
Is morally, ethic'ly

City Father No. 1
Spiritually, physically

City Father No. 2
Positively, absolutely

All the City Fathers
Undeniably and reliably
DEAD!

Glinda smiles.

Coroner (*walking up steps with a huge death certificate
and singing*)
As Coroner, I must aver,
I thoroughly examined her,
And she's not only merely dead,
She's really most sincerely dead.

Mayor
Then this is a day of independence
For all the Munchkins and their descendants –

Barrister (*pompously*)
If any!

Mayor
Yes, let the joyous news be spread
The wicked old witch at last is dead!

*They all cheer and dance. Camera pans during the next
lines showing the Munchkins happily spreading the glad
news.*

All Munchkins (*singing*)
Ding Dong, the witch is dead
Which old witch?
The wicked witch
Ding Dong, the wicked witch is dead!

Wake up, you sleepy head
(Sleepy heads in a bird's nest wake up.)
Rub your eyes,
Get out of bed.
Wake up, the wicked witch is dead!
She's gone where the goblins go
Below, below, below,
Yo ho let's open up and sing,
And ring the bells out:
Ding Dong! the merry-o
Sing it high,
Sing it low,
Let them know
The wicked witch is dead!

Munchkin Soldiers parade and march.

LONG SHOT – CIVIC CENTER

*Dorothy is standing on the steps as three Tiny Tots
dance through the line of Soldiers.*

Tiny Tots (*singing as they dance on tip-toe*)
We represent the Lullaby League, the Lullaby League,
    the Lullaby League,
And in the name of the Lullaby League,
We wish to welcome you to Munchkinland.

Dorothy blows a kiss.

Three Tough Kids now clog-hop up to Dorothy.

Tough Kids (*singing*)
We represent da Lollipop Guild, da Lollipop Guild, da
    Lollipop Guild
And in da name of da Lollipop Guild
We wish to welcome you to Munchkinland.

FULL SHOT – CIVIC CENTER

The three Tough Kids hand Dorothy a big lollipop.

Other Munchkins, the Mayor, the City Fathers,
   etc. (*singing*)
   We welcome you to Munchkinland
   Tra-la-la-la-la-la
   Tra-la-la, Tra-la-la
   (*little musical interlude*)
   Tra-la-la-la-la-la-la

Mayor (*to Dorothy*)
   From now on you'll be history

Barrister
   You'll be hist . . .

City Father
   You'll be hist . . .

Mayor
   You'll be history.

Group
   And we will glorify your name.

Mayor
   You will be a bust . . .

Barrister
   Be a bust . . .

City Father
   Be a bust . . .

Group
   In the Hall of Fame!

All Munchkins
   Tra-la-la-la-la-la,
   Tra-la-la, Tra-la-la
   Tra-la-la-la-la-la-la –
   Tra-la-la-la-la-la

Tra-la-la, Tra-la-la
Tra-la-la-la-la-la-la
Tra-la-la-la-la, Tra-la-la, Tra-la-la-la
Tra-la-la-la-la-la —

Suddenly on the last tra-la, the music stops with a terrific explosion followed by a burst of red smoke in front of Dorothy's house.

The Munchkins scatter and some fall flat on their faces with a wail of terror.

CLOSE SHOT – THE WICKED WITCH

The smoke clears away, leaving the Witch of the West standing facing Camera.

CLOSE-UP – DOROTHY

Terrified, she hugs Toto close to her.

CLOSE SHOT – THE WICKED WITCH

She walks over to the farmhouse to look at the Wicked Witch of the East.

MEDIUM SHOT – DOROTHY – GLINDA

Dorothy (*in alarm and bewilderment*) I thought you said she was dead!

Glinda That was her sister, the Wicked Witch of the East. This is the Wicked Witch of the West. And she's worse than the other one was.

MEDIUM SHOT – THE WICKED WITCH

She turns away from the farmhouse. Camera pans as she turns to Glinda and Dorothy.

Witch Who killed my sister? Who killed the Witch of the East? (*to Dorothy*) Was it *you*?

Dorothy (*fearfully*) No. No! It was an accident – I didn't mean to kill anybody!

Witch Well, my little pretty, I can cause accidents, too!

Glinda (*quickly*) Aren't you forgetting the ruby slippers?

Witch The slippers – yes, the slippers!
(*She hurries to the house and is just about to snatch up the slippers when they vanish from under her hands and the feet shrivel up under the house.*)
They're gone! The ruby slippers – what have you done with them?
Give them back to me or I'll – (*turning back to Glinda*)

Glinda It's too late!
(*She points her wand at Dorothy's feet.*)
There they are, and there they'll stay!

CLOSE-UP – DOROTHY'S FEET

In the ruby slippers.

Dorothy Oh!

CLOSE SHOT – WITCH, GLINDA, DOROTHY

Witch (*to both Glinda and Dorothy, in a frenzy*) Give me back my slippers! I'm the only one that knows how to use them – they're of no use to you! – Give them back to me – give them back!

Glinda (*to Dorothy*) Keep tight inside of them – their magic must be very powerful, or she wouldn't want them so badly!

Witch (*furiously*) You stay out of this, Glinda, or I'll fix you as well!

33

Glinda (*laughs*) Oh, ho-ho, rubbish! You have no power here! Be gone before somebody drops a house on you, too!

Witch (*falling back as she looks up*) Very well – I'll bide my time –
(*to Dorothy*) – and as for you, my fine lady, it's true I can't attend to you here and now as I'd like; but just try to stay out of my way – just try! I'll get you, my pretty, and your little dog, too!
(*With a burst of laughter, she whirls around and vanishes in a burst of smoke and fire and a clap of thunder.*)

MEDIUM SHOT – GLINDA, DOROTHY

Glinda (*to the Munchkins*) It's all right – you can get up. She's gone. It's all right. You can all get up.

LONG SHOT – THE MUNCHKINS

They rise to their feet and dust themselves off sheepishly.

CLOSE SHOT – GLINDA AND DOROTHY

Glinda (*daintily*) Ooh, what a smell of sulfur!
(*to Dorothy*) I'm afraid you've made rather a bad enemy of the Wicked Witch of the West. The sooner you get out of Oz altogether, the safer you'll sleep, my dear.

Dorothy Oh, I'd give anything to get out of Oz altogether; but which is the way back to Kansas? I can't go the way I came!

The Munchkins all shake their heads regretfully.

Glinda No, that's true. The only person who might know would be the great and wonderful Wizard of Oz himself.

All the Munchkins bow deeply at the name.

Dorothy (*noticing the Munchkins' reaction*) The Wizard of Oz? Is he good or is he wicked?

Glinda Oh, very good; but very mysterious. He lives in the Emerald City, and that's a long journey from here. Did you bring your broomstick with you?

Dorothy No, I'm afraid I didn't.

Glinda Well, then, you'll have to walk. The Munchkins will see you safely to the border of Munchkinland. And remember, never let those ruby slippers off your feet for a moment, or you will be at the mercy of the Wicked Witch of the West. (*Kisses her on forehead.*)

Dorothy But how do I start for Emerald City?

Glinda It's always best to start at the beginning. And all you do is follow the Yellow Brick Road. (*pointing with wand*)

PAN SHOT

Dorothy walks forward.

Dorothy But what happens if I –

MEDIUM SHOT – THE COUNTRYSIDE FROM DOROTHY'S VIEWPOINT

Glinda Just follow the Yellow Brick Road.

She steps back, and the large pink-tinted crystal bubble reappears. The bubble slowly rises, carrying Glinda away, as the Munchkins rush toward it.

Munchkins Good-bye! Good-bye! Good-bye! (*etc.*)

MEDIUM SHOT – DOROTHY

Dorothy My! People come and go so quickly here!

The Munchkins laugh.

Camera pans down to Dorothy's ruby slippers as she steps onto the Yellow Brick Road.

Dorothy Follow the Yellow Brick Road. Follow the Yellow Brick Road?

Mayor Follow the Yellow Brick Road.

Munchkin Man Follow the Yellow Brick Road.

Munchkin Woman Follow the Yellow Brick Road.

Barrister Follow the Yellow Brick Road.

All Munchkins (*singing*)
Follow the Yellow Brick Road
Follow the Yellow Brick Road,
Follow, follow, follow, follow,
Follow the Yellow Brick Road.
Follow the Yellow Brick,
Follow the Yellow Brick,
Follow the Yellow Brick Road.

Five Little Fiddlers dance out behind Dorothy and lead the procession of Munchkins behind her and Toto.

You're off to see the Wizard,
The Wonderful Wizard of Oz.
You'll find he is a Whiz of a Wiz,
If ever a Wiz there was.
If ever, oh ever a Wiz there was,
The Wizard of Oz
Is one becoz
Becoz, becoz, becoz, becoz, becoz
Becoz of the wonderful things he does.
You're off to see the Wizard,
The Wonderful Wizard of Oz.

The quaint little procession marches off as Dorothy skips

*down the Yellow Brick Road. The Five Fiddlers play all
the way until they reach the boundary of Munchkinland.*

LONG SHOT – BOUNDARY

*Yellow Brick Road in foreground and hills and
fields in background. As the Munchkins finish their song,
they wave and call cheery good-byes. Dorothy turns and
waves good-bye and continues on her way.*

LAP DISSOLVE TO:
TRUCK SHOT – DOROTHY

*She is walking along the Yellow Brick Road. Toto is
trotting beside her. She stops as the Yellow Brick Road
crosses another one. She looks up and down, puzzled.*

Dorothy Follow the Yellow Brick Road, follow the
Yellow – Now which way do we go?

Voice Pardon me. That way is a very nice way.

LONG SHOT – SCARECROW

*He is hanging awkwardly on the pole, with his arm
pointing to the right down the road. His painted face
strangely resembles our old friend Hunk's.*

Dorothy Who said that?

CLOSE-UP – DOROTHY

*She looks around for the voice. Toto barks at the
Scarecrow.*

Dorothy Don't be silly, Toto. Scarecrows don't talk.

Scarecrow (*pointing to the left*) It's pleasant down that
way, too.

Dorothy (*to Toto*) That's funny. Wasn't he pointing the
other way?

Scarecrow (*now pointing in both directions*) Of course, people do go both ways!

Dorothy Why, you *did* say something, didn't you?

The Scarecrow shakes his head, then stops and nods it instead.

Are you doing that on purpose – or can't you make up your mind?

Scarecrow That's the trouble. I can't make up my mind. I haven't got a brain – only straw. (*showing her*)

Dorothy How can you talk if you haven't got a brain?

Scarecrow I don't know. But some people without brains do an awful lot of talking, don't they?

Dorothy (*speculatively*) Yes – I guess you're right. (*impressed by such a truth*) Well, we haven't really met properly, have we?

Scarecrow Why, no.

Dorothy (*curtsying*) How do you do?

Scarecrow (*nodding politely*) How do you do?

Dorothy Very well, thank you.

Scarecrow Oh, I'm not feeling at all well. You see, it's very tedious being stuck up here all day long with a pole up your back.

Dorothy Oh, dear! That must be terribly uncomfortable. Can't you get down?

Scarecrow Down? (*trying to reach in back of him*) No. You see, I'm – well, I'm –

Dorothy (*to his assistance*) Oh, well, here – let me help you!

Scarecrow Oh, that's very kind of you – very kind.

Dorothy (*puzzled – as she works*) Well, oh, dear – I don't quite see how I can –

Scarecrow Of course, I'm not bright about doing things, but if you'll just bend the nail down in the back, maybe I'll slip off and come –

Dorothy (*bending down the nail*) Oh yes!

Scarecrow (*as he slips off to the ground*) Ohhhh!
(*As he lands, his coat bursts open, and straw falls out from his abdomen.*)
Whoops! (*laughs*) There goes some of me again!

Dorothy (*horrified*) Oh! Does it hurt you?

Scarecrow (*blithely*) Oh, no. I just keep picking it up and putting it back in again.
(*He stuffs the straw back into his coat. He gets up and stretches himself luxuriously.*)

Dorothy Oh!

Scarecrow My! It's good to be free!
(*He whirls around and promptly falls over a broken fence rail.*)

Dorothy Oh! (*screams*) Ohhh! Oh!

Scarecrow (*sitting up with a hopeful smile*) Did I scare you?

Dorothy No, no. I – I just thought you hurt yourself.

Scarecrow But I didn't scare you . . .?

Dorothy (*as practical as Kansas*) No, of course not.

Scarecrow (*dolefully*) I didn't think so.

A crow lights on his shoulder at this moment.

Boo! Scat! Boo!

39

The crow picks a piece of straw and flies off with it.

(*to Dorothy*) You see, I can't even scare a crow! They come from miles around just to eat in my field and . . . and laugh in my face.
(*almost weeps*) Oh, I'm a *failure*, because I haven't got a brain!

Dorothy Well, what would you do with a brain if you had one?

Scarecrow Do? Why, if I had a brain I could –
(*goes into his song and amusing dance*)
I could while away the hours
Conferrin' with the flowers
Consultin' with the rain
And my head, I'd be scratchin'
While my thoughts were busy hatchin'
If I only had a brain.

Dorothy helps him up.

I'd unravel ev'ry riddle
For any individ'le
In trouble or in pain

Dorothy (*singing*)
With the thoughts you'd be thinkin'
You could be another Lincoln,
If you only had a brain.

Scarecrow (*singing*)
Oh, I could tell you why
The ocean's near the shore,
I could think of things I never thunk before
And then I'd sit and think some more.

I would not be just a nuffin'
My head all full of stuffin'
My heart all full of pain.

I would dance and be merry
Life would be a ding-a-derry
If I only had a brain – Whoa!

At the finish, he falls to the road. Dorothy picks up some of his straw and rushes over to him to stuff it back in again.

Dorothy Wonderful! (*shaking his hand*) Why, if our scarecrow back in Kansas could do that, the crows'd be scared to pieces!

Scarecrow They would?

Dorothy Hmm.

Scarecrow Where's Kansas?

Dorothy That's where I live. And I want to get back there so badly, I'm going all the way to Emerald City to get the Wizard of Oz to help me.

Scarecrow You're going to see a wizard?

Dorothy Um-hmmm.

Scarecrow (*with a sudden idea*) Do you think if I went with you, this Wizard would give me some brains?

Dorothy I couldn't say. (*then practically*) But even if he didn't, you'd be no worse off than you are now.

Scarecrow Yes, that's true.

Dorothy But maybe you better not. I've got a witch mad at me, and you might get into trouble.

Scarecrow Witch? Hmm! I'm not afraid of a witch. I'm not afraid of anything–
(*in a whisper with a look around*) – oh, except a lighted match. (*Touches his straw.*)

Dorothy (*in a low voice*) I don't blame you for that.

Scarecrow (*tensely*) But I'd face a whole box full of them

41

for the chance of getting some brains. (*pleading*) Look, I won't be any trouble, because I don't eat a thing; and I won't try to manage things, because I can't think. Uh . . . won't you take me with you?

Dorothy (*warmly*) Why, of *course*, I will!

Scarecrow (*leaping into the air*) Hooray! We're off to see a wizard! (*sinking down on her*)

Dorothy (*holding him up with difficulty*) Oh, well, you're not starting out very well.

Scarecrow Oh, I'll try – really I will.

Dorothy To Oz!

Scarecrow To Oz!

They link arms and go into Marching Song.

Dorothy and Scarecrow (*singing*)
We're off to see the Wizard,
The Wonderful Wizard of Oz.
We hear he is a Whiz of a Wiz
If ever a Wiz there was.
If ever, oh ever a Wiz there was,
The Wizard of Oz
Is one becoz
Becoz, becoz, becoz, becoz, becoz
Becoz of the wonderful things he does.
We're off to see the Wizard,
The Wonderful Wizard of Oz.

LAP DISSOLVE TO:
LONG SHOT – THE YELLOW BRICK ROAD

Running between fields and orchards. Along the road come Dorothy and the Scarecrow. They halt beside some old, gnarled apple trees with twisted branches laden with large red apples. Camera trucks to show that the Witch is in the shadows behind one of the trees. She slinks away.

Dorothy Oh, apples! Oh . . . look! Oh! Oh!

MEDIUM SHOT – DOROTHY AND TREES

She picks an apple. At once the end of the branch seizes the apple in a clawlike grab and takes it back, and the other slaps Dorothy's hand.

Dorothy Ouch!

First Tree What do you think you're doing?

Dorothy We've been walking a long ways, and I was hungry and – (*Suddenly, she blinks*). Did you say something?

First Tree (*to Second Tree*) She was hungry!

Second Tree She was hungry!

First Tree (*back to Dorothy*) Well, how would you like to have someone come along and pick something off of you?

Dorothy (*woefully*) Oh, dear! I keep forgetting I'm not in Kansas.

Scarecrow Come along, Dorothy, you don't want any of *those* apples. Hmmm!

First Tree Are you hinting my apples aren't what they ought to be?

Scarecrow Oh, no! It's just that she doesn't like little green *worms*!

First Tree Oh, you! (*grabbing Dorothy, who screams*)

The Scarecrow fights the tree as she struggles free.

43

Second Tree You can't do that to me!

Scarecrow (*to Dorothy*) I'll show you how to get apples.

He puts his thumbs in his ears and waggles his fingers at them.

First Tree takes an apple, swings its branch like a pitcher, and throws an apple at the Scarecrow and knocks him down. The Second Tree follows suit.

Dorothy Oh! Oh!

LONG SHOT – SCARECROW

He runs away from the trees, with apples pelting after him. Dorothy runs after him out of the way.

Scarecrow Aha! Hooray (*He begins picking them up.*) I guess that did it! Help yourself!

MEDIUM SHOT – DOROTHY (THE TIN MAN'S LITTLE COTTAGE IN BACKGROUND) – PAN SHOT

She runs to gather up the apples and falls on her hands and knees to pick one up. Camera is now in:

CLOSE SHOT

As Dorothy's hand closes in on the apple, she sees a tin foot just beside it. She raps on it and then looks up, and the Camera pans slowly up the figure of the Tin Man. His face, strangely enough, looks just like Hickory's.

MEDIUM SHOT – DOROTHY, TIN MAN

She scrambles to her feet, examining him.

Dorothy (*raps on him*) Why, it's a man! A man made out of tin!

Scarecrow What?

Dorothy Yes! Oh, look! (*She raps on his chest.*)

A *creaky, rusty sound comes from the Tin Man.*

Tin Man (*almost inaudibly*) Oil can! Oil can!

Dorothy (*to Tin Man*) Did you say something?

Tin Man (*still in a hoarse creak*) Oil can!

Dorothy He said oil can!

Scarecrow Oil can what?

Dorothy Oil can? Oh! Oh!

Tin Man Ahh . . .

Dorothy (*finding oil can*) Here it is! Where do you want to be oiled first?

Tin Man My mouth . . . my mouth!

Scarecrow He said his mouth!
(*He oils the Tin Man's mouth and hands the oil can to Dorothy.*)
The other side!

Dorothy Yes . . .
(*Dorothy sends a drop or two by the Tin Man's mouth.*)

Tin Man (*clearing his throat, as his joints squeak*) M–m–my, my, my, my, my, my, my goodness! I can talk again! Oh, oil my arms, please! Oil my elbows! Oh! Oh!

Dorothy (*as she takes the can from Scarecrow and starts working on the Tin Man's arm joints*) Here.

Tin Man Oh! Oh!

The Scarecrow oils the other arm.

Dorothy (*lowering the Tin Man's ax*) Oh.

Tin Man Oh!

Dorothy Did that hurt?

Tin Man No, it feels wonderful! I've held that ax up for ages. Oh!

Dorothy Goodness! How did you ever get like this?

Tin Man Oh, well, 'bout a year ago, I was chopping that tree, when suddenly it began to rain.

Dorothy Oh!

Tin Man And right in the middle of a chop, I – I rusted solid. I've been that way ever since. Oh.

As he talks, the Scarecrow and Dorothy are working his joints.

Dorothy Well, you're perfect now.

Tin Man (*to Scarecrow*) My – my neck! My – my neck! (*back to Dorothy*) Perfect? Oh, bang on my chest if you think I'm perfect. Go ahead – bang on it!

Dorothy raps on his chest, which echoes.

Scarecrow Beautiful! What an echo!

Tin Man It's empty.
(*He looks around, then lowers his voice as though telling a terrible secret.*)
The tinsmith forgot to give me a heart.

Dorothy and Scarecrow No heart?

Tin Man No heart!

Dorothy Oh.

Tin Man All hollow!
(*He bangs on his chest and knocks himself against a tree stump. They go to help him, but he holds them off.*)

46

(*singing*)
When a man's an empty kettle
He should be on his mettle
And yet I'm torn apart
Just because I'm presumin'
That I could be kind-a human
If I only had a heart.

I'd be tender, I'd be gentle
And awful sentimental
Regarding love and art
I'd be friends with the sparrows
And the boy who shoots the arrows,
If I only had a heart.
(*standing*)

Picture me . . . a balcony . . .
Above a voice sings low –

Snow White's Voice (*comes in singing*)
Wherefore art thou, Romeo?

Tin Man
(*two beats*) I hear a beat.
(*two beats*) How sweet!
Just to register emotion.
'Jealousy', 'devotion'
And really feel the part
I could stay young and chipper
And I'd lock it with a zipper
If I only had a heart.

*He goes into a dance. As the number finishes, Dorothy
and the Scarecrow are having a whispered conversation.
Just as he finishes, the Tin Man's joints lock, and
Dorothy and the Scarecrow come over to help. The
Tin Man staggers back with Dorothy and knocks the
Scarecrow over.*

Dorothy Oh, oh . . .

Tin Man (*landing on tree stump*) Oh!

Dorothy . . . oh, oh, oh, are you all right?

Tin Man I'm afraid I'm a little rusty yet. Oh.

Dorothy Oh, dear. That was wonderful! You know, we were just wondering why you couldn't come with us to the Emerald City to ask the Wizard of Oz for a heart!

Tin Man Well, suppose the Wizard wouldn't give me one when we got there?

Dorothy Oh, but he will! (*in distress*) He must! We've come such a long way already –

A wild peal of laughter.

Camera pans up to roof of Tin Man's cottage, and perched on the roof is the Wicked Witch.

Witch You call that *long*? Why, you've just begun! Helping the little lady along, are you, my fine gentlemen? Well, stay away from her! (*savagely to the Scarecrow*) Or I'll stuff a mattress with you!

MEDIUM SHOT – THREE

The Scarecrow winces. The Tin Man points to him and then to himself.

Witch And *you*! I'll use you for a beehive! Here, Scarecrow! Want to play ball?
(*She throws down a ball of fire with a scream of laughter.*)

LONG SHOT – THREE

The ball of fire drops down in front of the Scarecrow, and he leaps wildly in terror. Dorothy screams.

48

Scarecrow Oh! Look out! Fire! I'm burning! I'm burning! Oh! Take it away!

The Tin Man slams his tin hat down on the fireball to put it out.

LONG SHOT – WITCH

On roof she laughs again and vanishes in a puff of red smoke.

CLOSE-UP – DOROTHY

With Toto in her arms, as smoke clears.

MEDIUM SHOT – THREE

The Scarecrow gets up from the ground. The Tin Man puts his hat on again.

Scarecrow (*angrily*) I'm not afraid of her! I'll see you get safely to the Wizard now. Whether I get a brain or not! Stuff a mattress with me! Heh!
(*He snaps his fingers.*)

Tin Man (*heartily*) I'll see you reach the Wizard, whether I get a heart or not! Beehive! Bah! Let her try and make a beehive out of me!
(*He snaps his fingers.*)

Dorothy (*happily*) Oh, you're the best friends anybody ever had! And it's funny, but I feel as if I've known you all the time – but I couldn't have, could I?

Scarecrow I don't see how. You weren't around when I was stuffed and sewn together, were you?

Tin Man And I was standing over there, rusting for the longest time.

Dorothy (*still puzzled*) Still – I wish I could remember . . . but I guess it doesn't matter, anyway – we know each other now, don't we?

49

Scarecrow That's right.

Tin Man We do!

They all laugh.

Scarecrow (*offering his arm to Dorothy*) To Oz!

Tin Man (*offering his arm to her*) To Oz!

They march off, singing. Toto runs out and joins them.

Dorothy, Tin Man and Scarecrow
We're off to see the Wizard,
The Wonderful Wizard of Oz.
We hear he is a Whiz of a Wiz
If ever a Wiz there was.
If ever, oh ever a Wiz there was,
The Wizard of Oz
Is one becoz
Becoz, becoz, becoz, becoz, becoz
Becoz of the wonderful things he does.
We're off to see the Wizard,
The Wonderful Wizard of Oz.

LAP DISSOLVE TO:
LONG SHOT – A DARK AND EERIE FOREST

The comrades are coming along the Yellow Brick Road.

They move forward slowly and stop.

Dorothy Oh, I don't like this forest! It's – it's dark and creepy!

Scarecrow Of course, I don't know, but I think it'll get darker before it gets lighter.

Dorothy Do – do you suppose we'll meet any wild animals?

Tin Man Mmm – we might.

Dorothy Oh –

Scarecrow Animals that – that eat straw?

Tin Man (*nonchalantly*) Uh, some. But mostly lions and tigers and bears.

Dorothy Lions?

Scarecrow And tigers?

Tin Man (*nodding*) And bears.

Dorothy Oh! Lions and tigers and bears. Oh my!

LONG SHOT – THREE

They look around and slowly start to run.

All (*reciting in rhythm to their steps, each time louder and faster*) Lions and tigers and bears!

Dorothy Oh my!

All Lions and tigers and bears!

Dorothy Oh my!

All Lions and tigers and bears!

Dorothy Oh my!

All Lions and tigers and bears!

Dorothy Oh my!

A roar from ahead of them.

Scarecrow (*pointing*) Oh, look!

Dorothy Oh!

LONG SHOT – COWARDLY LION

In distance he roars. He advances; they retreat. He advances; they retreat. He advances; they retreat. He

51

leaps in the air and comes down on all fours, scattering the others. He straightens up in a boxer's stance and then waltzes menacingly, doing some very fancy shadow-boxing.

Lion (*growling*) Hah, put 'em up, put 'em up! Which one of ya first? I'll fight ya both together if ya want. I'll fight ya with one paw tied behind my back. (*Puts paw behind back.*) I'll fight ya standin' on one foot! (*Stands on one foot.*) I'll fight ya with my eyes closed. (*Closes his eyes, then opens them – to Tin Man*) Ohhhh – pullin' an ax on me, eh? (*to Scarecrow*) Sneakin' up on me, eh? Why . . . (*Growls.*)

Tin Man Here, here. Go 'way and let us alone.

Lion Oh, scared, huh? Afraid, huh? Ha! How long can ya stay fresh in that can? (*Laughs.*) Come on! Get up and fight, ya shiverin' junkyard. (*to Scarecrow*) Put ya hands up, ya lopsided bag of hay!

Scarecrow (*reproachfully*) Now, that's getting personal, Lion!

Tin Man Yes, get up and teach him a lesson!

Scarecrow Well, what's wrong with you teachin' him?

Tin Man Ah – well – well, I hardly know him.

CLOSE SHOT – TOTO

Barking.

Lion I'll get you anyway, peewee! (*Growls.*)

Dorothy No!

Toto jumps into the bushes with the Lion growling after him. Dorothy grabs Toto in her arms. She slaps the Lion smartly on the nose.

Shame on you!

Lion (*bawling*) What did ya do that for? I didn't bite him!

Dorothy No, but you *tried* to! It's bad enough picking on a straw man, but when you go around picking on poor little dogs –

Lion (*sniffing pathetically*) Well, ya didn't have to go and hit me, did ya? Is my nose bleedin'? (*sobbing*)

Dorothy (*severely*) Well, of course not! My goodness, what a fuss you're making! Well, naturally when you go around picking on things weaker than you are – why, you're nothing but a great big coward!

Lion (*to Dorothy, with great self-pity, playing with his tail*) You're right, I *am* a coward! I haven't any courage at all! I even scare myself. Look at the circles under my eyes! I haven't slept in weeks!

Tin Man Why don't you try counting sheep?

Lion That doesn't do any good – I'm afraid of 'em! (*bawling*)

Scarecrow Oh, that's too bad. (*to Dorothy*) Don't you think the Wizard could help him, too?

Dorothy I don't see why not. (*to Lion*) Why don't you come along with us? We're on our way to see the Wizard now. (*pointing to the Tin Man*) To get him a heart.

Tin Man (*pointing to the Scarecrow*) And him a brain.

Dorothy I'm sure he could give you some courage!

Lion Well, wouldn't you feel degraded to be seen in the company of a cowardly lion? *I* would. (*sobbing*)

Dorothy No, of course not!

Lion (*still sniffling*) Gee, that – that's awfully nice of ya. My life has been simply unbearable.

Dorothy Oh, well, it's all right now. The Wizard'll fix everything.

Lion (*emotionally as they walk*) It – It's been in me so long, I just gotta tell ya how I feel.

Dorothy (*taking his arm*) Well, come on!

Lion (*singing*)
Yeah, it's sad, believe me, missy,
When you're born to be a sissy,
Without the vim and verve.
But I could show my prowess,
Be a lion not a mowess,
If I only had the nerve.

I'm afraid there's no denyin'
I'm just a dandelion,
A fate I don't deserve.
I'd be brave as a blizzard . . .

Tin Man (*singing*)
I'd be gentle as a lizard . . .

Scarecrow (*singing*)
I'd be clever as a gizzard . . .

Dorothy (*singing*)
If the Wizard is a wizard who will serve.

Scarecrow (*singing*)
Then I'm sure to get a brain . . .

Tin Man (*singing*)
. . . a heart

Dorothy (*singing*)
. . . a home

Lion (*singing*)
. . . the nerve!

All (*singing, arm in arm*)
   Oh, we're off to see the Wizard,
   The Wonderful Wizard of Oz.
   We hear he is a Whiz of a Wiz
   If ever a Wiz there was.
   If ever, oh ever a Wiz there was,
   The Wizard of Oz
   Is one becoz
   Becoz, becoz, becoz, becoz, becoz
   Becoz of the wonderful things he does.
   We're off to see the Wizard,
   The Wonderful Wizard of Oz.

MUSICAL FADE OUT

CLOSE-UP – CRYSTAL

*In it we see the four friends marching arm in arm.
Camera pulls back to show the Witch of the West
gazing into it and laughing. Near her sits her familiar
winged chimpanzee, Nikko, watching the crystal.*

Witch (*laughing*) Aha, so you won't take warning, eh? All
the worse for you, then – I'll take care of you now instead
of later! Hah!
(*She turns, mixes poison, and returns to crystal.*)
When I gain those ruby slippers, my power will be the
greatest in Oz!
(*holding poison over crystal*) And now, my beauties! . . .
something with poison in it, I think; with poison in it, but
attractive to the eye and soothing to the smell! Heh, heh,
heh, heh, heh, heh!
(*The poppy field fades into the crystal as she runs her
fingers over it.*)
Poppies . . . poppies . . . poppies will put them to
sleep . . . sleep . . . now they'll sleep . . .

DISSOLVE TO:
LONG SHOT – POPPY FIELD

Camera pans over the field to the four in the far distance, marching.

MEDIUM SHOT – FOUR

They suddenly halt.

Dorothy (*pointing*) There's Emerald City!

LONG SHOT – EMERALD CITY

Shooting across the poppy field. In the far distance stands the glittering towers and domes of the Emerald City.

Dorothy (*in rapture*) Oh, we're almost there at last! At last!

CLOSE SHOT – FOUR

Dorothy It's beautiful, isn't it? Just like I knew it would be! He really must be a wonderful wizard to live in a city like that!

Lion Well, come on, then. What are we waiting for?

Scarecrow Nothing! Let's hurry!

Dorothy Yes, let's run!

Lion Yeah!

They all run into the poppy field. The Scarecrow and Tin Man quickly run on ahead as the Cowardly Lion and Dorothy lag behind.

Scarecrow Come on! Come on!

Tin Man Hurry! Hurry!

Scarecrow Oh, look!

LONG SHOT – EMERALD CITY

With Yellow Brick Road beyond poppies.

LONG SHOT – POPPY FIELD

Tin Man Oh!

Scarecrow Come on!

Tin Man Look! You can see it here! It's wonderful! Emerald City!

Camera pans with Dorothy as she struggles through the poppies. A puzzled look comes on her face.

Dorothy (*panting*) Oh . . . oh, what's happening? What is it? (*putting her hand to her forehead*) I can't run anymore . . . I'm so sleepy . . .

Scarecrow Here, give us your hands and we'll pull you along.

Dorothy Oh, no, please – I have to rest for just a minute. Toto . . . where's Toto?

CLOSE-UP – TOTO

He is fast asleep.

LONG SHOT – POPPY FIELD

Dorothy sinks down and falls asleep.

Scarecrow Oh, you can't rest now. We're nearly there.

CLOSE-UP – TIN MAN

He begins to cry.

FULL SHOT – THREE

Standing around Dorothy.

Scarecrow (*to Tin Man*) Don't cry – you'll rust yourself again!

Lion (*slowly sinking down*) Comin' to think of it forty winks (*Yawns.*) wouldn't be bad . . . (*Yawns.*)

Scarecrow Don't you start it, too!

The Scarecrow and Tin Man grab his arms and stand him up again.

Tin Man No! We ought to try and carry Dorothy.

Scarecrow I don't think I could . . . but we could try.

Tin Man Let's.

Scarecrow Yes.

They both let go of the Lion so they can help Dorothy. He falls behind them flat on his back, fast asleep.

Tin Man (*seeing Lion*) Oh, now look at him! This is terrible!

Scarecrow Here, Tin Man – help me.

Tin Man Oh!

Scarecrow (*trying to lift Dorothy*) Uh! Oh, this is terrible! Can't budge her an inch!
(*looking to Tin Man*) This is a spell, this is!

Tin Man It's the Wicked Witch! What'll we do? HELP! HELP! (*beginning to cry*)

Scarecrow It's no use screaming at a time like this! Nobody will hear you! HELP! HELP! HELP!

LONG SHOT – TIN MAN AND SCARECROW

In poppy field.

Suddenly the theme music of the Good Witch fades in

*softly, and the next moment the sky is full of falling
snowflakes. Superimposed through this scene we see
faintly the face of Glinda as she waves her wand – to
get across the fact that Glinda has answered their
call.*

Scarecrow HELP! HELP! HELP! (*now looking up in
wonder*) It's snowing!

CLOSE-UP – DOROTHY WITH TOTO IN HER ARMS

Asleep, as the snow begins settling on her.

LONG SHOT – TIN MAN AND SCARECROW

*Superimposed with close-up of Glinda as she waves her
wand. Snow still falling.*

Scarecrow No, it isn't! Yes, it is! Oh, maybe that'll help!
Oh, but it couldn't help!

CLOSE-UP – DOROTHY

She stirs slightly and opens her eyes.

Scarecrow Does help! Dorothy, you're waking up!

Dorothy (*rising*) Oh . . . oh . . .

Lion (*sitting up*) Ah – ah. Unusual weather we're havin',
ain't we?

They laugh.

Dorothy (*pointing to Tin Man*) Look, he's rusted again!
Oh, give me the oil can, quick!

Scarecrow (*handing it to her*) Here! Oh! Here!

Dorothy (*oiling his joints*) Oh, quick! Oh!

Scarecrow He is rusted! Here!

Dorothy Here! Oh! Oh, quick! Oh! Oh!

INT. CLOSE-UP – TOWER ROOM

Their images in crystal. Camera pulls back to Witch and Nikko as the picture fades.

Witch (*furiously*) Curseit! Curseit! Somebody always helps that girl!

Nikko hands her the wishing cap.

But shoes or no shoes . . . I'm still great enough to conquer her! And woe to those who try to stop me! (*She flings it furiously across the room.*)

LAP DISSOLVE TO:
FULL SHOT – THE FOUR

Dorothy Come on, let's get out of here. Look – Emerald City is closer and prettier than ever!

They link arms and tramp out of the snow-covered field as they hear a chorus of voices offscreen begin to sing.

Optimistic Voices (*out of the air – singing*)
You're out of the woods
You're out of the dark
You're out of the night

Step into the sun
Step into the light
Keep straight ahead for
The most glor . . .
. . . ious place
On the face
Of the earth or the sky

LONG SHOT – THE EMERALD CITY

They go skipping arm in arm down the Yellow Brick Road.

Optimistic Voices
Hold onto your breath
Hold onto your heart
Hold onto your hope
March up to the gate
And bid it open –

LAP DISSOLVE TO:
MEDIUM SHOT – INT. TOWER ROOM – WITCH
AND NIKKO

She grabs her broomstick and laughs, going to window.

Witch Ha! (*laughing*) To the Emerald City as fast as lightning!

LONG SHOT – EXT. TOWER

Camera pans with Witch as she flies away on her broomstick, laughing wildly.

LAP DISSOLVE TO:
LONG SHOT – GATE TO THE EMERALD CITY

The Four are skipping up to the gate.

Optimistic Voices (*singing*)
You're out of the woods
You're out of the dark
You're out of the night

Step into the sun
Step into the light
March up to the gate
And bid it open! – open!

MEDIUM SHOT – THE FOUR AT THE GATE

Dorothy rings the bell. A little window in the door opens.

CLOSE SHOT – THE WINDOW

Out pops a head with a round face. Although he now wears a mustache, something about the head is strangely reminiscent of our old friend, Professor Marvel.

Doorman (*fiercely*) Who rang that bell?

MEDIUM SHOT – THE FOUR

All (*together*) We did!

Doorman (*still more severely*) Can't you read?

Scarecrow Read what?

Doorman The notice!

All (*together*) What notice?

Doorman It's on the door – as plain as the nose on my face! It's ah – oh – oh – oh – oh.
(*He cranes his head out, clucks with annoyance, vanishes, and his hand immediately reappears with a card, which he hangs out of the window, and then slams it shut.*)

All (*reading card*) 'Bell out of order. Please knock.'

Dorothy then knocks. The window opens once more, and the Doorman's face reappears.

Doorman Well, that's more like it! Now, state your business.

All (*together*) We want to see the Wizard!

Doorman (*so shocked that he almost falls*) Oh – oh – the Wizard? Ah – but nobody can see the Great Oz!

Nobody's ever seen the Great Oz! Even *I've* never seen him!

Dorothy (*guilelessly*) Well, then, how do you know there is one?

Doorman Because – he . . . ah . . . b – I – oh – (*unable to think of a good reason*) You're wasting my time!

Dorothy Oh, please – please, sir – I've *got* to see the Wizard. The Good Witch of the North sent me.

Doorman Prove it!

Scarecrow She's wearing the ruby slippers she gave her!

INSERT

Dorothy's ruby slippers.

Doorman Oh, so she is! Well, bust my buttons! Why didn't you say that in the first place? That's a horse of a different color! Come on in! (*Slams window.*)

LONG SHOT

As they come through the gates, we see the beautiful, glittering streets of Emerald City beyond them. As they enter, a buggy drawn by a white horse drives up. Strange as it may seem, the fat Cabby is also Professor Marvel, in an entirely different makeup and wearing a scrubby little beard and mustache. In this character he is as cockney as a costermonger.

Cabby (*as he drives up*) Cabby! Cabby! Just what you're looking for! Tyke you anywhere in the city, we does!

Dorothy (*as he looks down*) Well, would you take us to see the Wizard?

Cabby (*stalling*) The Wizard? The Wizard? . . . I . . .

can't . . . well, yes, of course . . . But first I'll tyke you to a little place where you can tidy up a bit, what?

Dorothy (*getting in, followed by others*) Oh, thank you, so much, we've been gone such a long time, and we feel so mess –

Camera pans to horse in foreground, showing that it now has turned to a beautiful shade of purple.

(*to Cabby*) What kind of a horse is *that*? I've never seen a horse like *that* before!

Cabby No, and never will again, I fancy! There's only one of him, and he's it. He's the Horse of a Different Color you've heard tell about! (*Laughs.*)

Cabby starts off. We carry them in a trucking shot through the street as the Cabby leads into his song.

Cabby and Citizens (*singing*)
Ha-ha-ha
Ho-ho-ho
And a couple of tra-la-las
That's how we laugh the day away
In the Merry Old Land of Oz
'Bzz-'bzz-'bzz
Chirp, chirp, chirp
And a couple of la-de-das.

The horse neighs and is now red.

That's how the crickets crick all day
In the Merry Old Land of Oz.
We get up at twelve and start to work at one,

The horse neighs and is now yellow

Take an hour for lunch, and then at two we're done,
Jolly good fun.

Ha-ha-ha!
Ho-ho-ho!
And a couple of tra-la-las,
That's how we laugh the day away,
In the Merry Old Land of Oz.
Ha-ha-ha
Ho-ho-ho

Cabby
Ha-ha-ha-ha!

Citizens
And a couple of tra-la-las

All
That's how we laugh the day away,
With a ho-ho-ho!
Ha-ha-ha!
In the Merry Old Land of Oz.

We synchronize end of song with arrival of Carriage in front of the magic washup parlor, with 'Wash & Brush Up Co.' over the door.

As the four get down, we go into a short musical montage (still using the song with a few new lines to point up the scenes).

The first eight bars are taken up by the Masseurs, who are filling the Scarecrow with new straw.

Masseurs (*singing*)
Pat, pat here,
Pat, pat there,
And a couple of brand-new strahz.
That's how we keep you young and fair
In the Merry Old Land of Oz.

Polishers shining up the Tin Man.

Polishers (*singing*)
  Rub, rub here,
  Rub, rub there,
  And whether you're tin or brahz.
  That's how we keep you in repair
  In the Merry Old Land of Oz.

  Dorothy at the Beauticians'.

Beautician (*singing*)
  We can make a dimpled smile out of a frown.

Dorothy
  Can you even dye my eyes to match my gown?

Beautician
  Uh-huh.

Dorothy
  Jolly old town!

  Manicurists fixing Lion's claws.

Manicurists (*singing*)
  Clip, clip here,
  Clip, clip there,
  We give the roughest clawzz –

Lion (*singing*)
  That certain air of savoir faire
  In the Merry Old Land of Oz! – Ha!

  The other three join him, all laughing.

Scarecrow
  Ha-ha-ha-

Tin Man
  Ho-ho-ho-

Dorothy
  Ha-ha-ha-ha-

Lion (*rising*)
  Ha!

All (*singing*)
  That's how we laugh the day away
  In the Merry Old Land of Oz

  As all Four are coming out into the City Square, the whole town is singing.

  That's how we laugh the day away
  And a ha-ha-ha
  Ha-ha-ha-ha-ha-ha
  Ha-ha-ha-ha-ha-ha-ha-ha-ha
  In the Merry Old Land of Oz
  Ha-ha-ha-ho-ho-ho – (*laughing*)

The Four
  We're off to see the Wizard
  The Wonderful Wizard of –

  There is a loud noise. All stop and look up, screaming.

LONG SHOT – SKY OVER CITY

  The Witch is flying overhead on her broomstick. She laughs as a long streak of black smoke trails out from behind and forms the letters: S–U–R–R

MEDIUM SHOT – FOUR

  Looking up.

Lion Who's her? Who's her?

Dorothy It's the Witch! She's followed us here!

LONG SHOT – SKY

  In smoke the Witch has written: SURRENDER DOROTHY

Lion 'Surrender Dorothy.'

Dorothy Oh!

Oz Woman No. 1 Dorothy? Who's Dorothy!

Oz Woman No. 2 The Wizard will explain it!

Oz Man No. 1 To the Wizard!

Oz Man No. 2 To the Wizard!

They are all rushing off.

Dorothy Dear, whatever shall we do?

Scarecrow Well, we'd better hurry if we're going to see the Wizard!

They run off with the rest of the crowd.

LONG SHOT – THE GATES OF THE PALACE

This is in front of the Palace of Oz, where there are flowers and steps going up to double doors. A crowd of townspeople is surrounding the gates, clamoring to see the Wizard.

In front of the gates stands a funny Guard, dressed in a tall shako and a costume that is a slightly exaggerated version of the English palace guards. He carries an extremely long gun with flowers in the barrel. Believe it or not, the Guard is Professor Marvel, with a fiercely turned-up mustache.

Guard (*bellowing at the mob*) Here – here! Here! Everything is all right. Stop that now – just – every – it's all right! Everything is all right! The Great and Powerful Oz has got matters well in hand – I hope – and so you can all go home! And there's nothing to worry about! Get out of here now – go on! Go on home, and I – I – Go home.

Dorothy and her friends make their way through the crowd.

Dorothy If you please, sir – we want to see the Wizard right away – all four of us!

Guard (*firmly*) Orders are: Nobody can see the Great Oz, not nobody, not nohow!

Dorothy Oh, but – but please. It's very important.

Lion And – and I got a permanent just for the occasion.

Guard Not nobody, not nohow!

Scarecrow But she's Dorothy!

Guard The Witch's Dorothy? Humph! Well, that makes a difference! Just wait here – I'll announce you at once!
(*He marches inside.*)

Scarecrow Did you hear that? He'll announce us at once! I've as good as got my brain!

Tin Man I can fairly hear my heart beating!

Dorothy I'll be home in time for supper!

Lion In another hour I'll be King of the Forest. Long live the King!
(*singing*)
If I were King of the Forest,
Not Queen, not Duke, not Prince.
My regal robes of the forest
Would be satin, not cotton, not chintz.
I'd command each thing, be it fish or fowl,
With a woof and a woof, and a royal growl – woof.
As I'd click my heel,
All the trees would kneel,
And the mountains bow,
And the bulls kowtow,
And the sparrow would take wing
'F – I . . . 'f . . . I . . . were King.

Each rabbit would show respect to me.
The chipmunks genuflect to me.
Though my tail would lash,
I would show compash
For every underling,
'F – I . . . 'f . . . I . . . were King –
Just King.

*Coronation ceremony to music. Business of laying
down carpet, Dorothy acting as flower girl and train
bearer picking up rug as a royal robe, and the Tin
Man breaking a flowerpot and crowning the Lion
with it.*

Lion (*singing*)
Monarch of all I survey
Mah-ah-ah-ah-ah-ah-ah-ah-ah-*narch*!
Of all I survey!

Dorothy and the Scarecrow bow.

Dorothy Your Majesty, if you were King, you wouldn't be
afraid of anything?

Lion Not nobody, not nohow!

Tin Man Not even a rhinocerous?

Lion Imposserous!

Dorothy How about a hippopotamus?

Lion Why, I'd thrash him from top to bottomus.

Dorothy Supposin' you met an elephant?

Lion I'd wrap him up in cellophant.

Scarecrow What if it were a brontosaurus?

Lion I'd show him who was King of the Fores'.

All How?

Lion

How? . . . Courage!
What makes a king out of a slave!
  . . . Courage!
What makes the flag on the mast to wave!
  . . . Courage!
What makes the elephant charge his tusk
In the misty mist or the dusky dusk?
What makes the muskrat guard his musk?
  . . . Courage!
What makes the sphinx the seventh wonder?
  . . . Courage!
What makes the dawn come up like thunder?
  . . . Courage!
What makes the Hottentot so hot?
What puts the 'ape' in apricot?
What have they got that I ain't got?

All Courage!

Lion You can say that again! Ha, ha – huh?

LONG SHOT – DOOR

The Guard comes out of the Palace.

Guard Ahhhhh! The Wizard says go away!
(*Exits, slamming door.*)

All (*in horror*) Go *away*?

Dorothy Oh –

Scarecrow (*mildly*) Looks like we came a long way for
nothing.

Dorothy (*really losing her courage for the first time*) Oh,
and I was so happy – (*Sits down on the steps.*) I thought I
was on my way home.

As she begins to cry, the others all start comforting her. The Scarecrow takes the handkerchief from her basket and hands it to her.

As she talks brokenly, the Guard is peering out the window in the door. He is beginning to be affected by the scene.

Tin Man Don't cry, Dorothy. We're going to get you to the Wizard.

Scarecrow We certainly are.

Dorothy (*who has been growing more and more unhappy*) Auntie Em was so good to me, and I never appreciated it . . . running away and hurting her feelings. Professor Marvel said she was sick. She may be dying! And it's all my fault.

CLOSE-UP – GUARD AT WINDOW

Tears trickle down his cheeks and drip off his mustache.

Dorothy Oh, I'll never forgive myself! Never – never – never!

Guard (*sobbing*) Oh, oh! Please don't cry anymore! I'll get you in to the Wizard somehow! Come on. I had an Aunt Em myself once.

He disappears, and the doors of the Palace open slowly. The four enter down a long corridor.

LONG SHOT – INT. PALACE CORRIDOR

It seems to stretch on forever, high and narrow, and has an awe-inspiring air of mystery and silence. Dorothy, the Tin Man, the Scarecrow and the Lion are walking down this corridor slowly, cautiously.

Lion (*stopping*) Wait a minute, fellas! I was just thinkin' – I really don't want to see the Wizard this much. I better wait for you outside.

He turns to go, but they stop him.

Scarecrow What's the matter?

Tin Man Oh, he's just scared again.

Dorothy (*reassuringly*) Don't you know the Wizard's going to give you some courage?

Lion (*twiddling his tail nervously, occasionally wiping away tears with the brush on the end*) I'd be too scared to ask him for it! (*bawling*)

Dorothy Oh, well, then we'll ask him *for* you!

Lion I'd sooner wait outside.

He turns to run, but they stop him.

Dorothy Why? Why?

Lion (*sobbing*) Because I'm still scared!

Dorothy Come on.

Lion (*absently tugs at his tail with his paws and gives a wail of fear*) Ow-oo!

Scarecrow (*as they turn*) What happened?

Lion (*bawling*) Somebody pulled my tail!

Scarecrow You did it yourself!

Lion (*looking at his paws*) I – oh –

Scarecrow Here . . . come on.

They all clasp hands.

Oz's Voice (*booming and echoing*) Come forward!

LONG SHOT – END OF CORRIDOR

Two huge doors swing open.

LONG SHOT – FOUR

They walk cautiously forward.

Lion (*clasping his paws over his eyes*) Tell me when it's over!

LONG SHOT – INT. THRONE ROOM – SHOOTING FROM THEIR ANGLE

It is a huge, lofty hall, beautifully decorated in green and silver glass. At the far end is a short flight of stairs leading to a huge throne. On the steps also are two silver urns, from which flames and smoke arise. A gigantic, shadowy head hovers above the throne.

Lion Look at that! Look at that! (*crying*) I want to go home!

Oz's Voice I am Oz, the Great and Powerful! Who are you?

LONG SHOT – FOUR

They are huddled together in an unhappy little group. The Lion is shivering. The rest are nudging Dorothy, indicating that she is to be the spokesperson. In the end they shove her forward.

Oz's Voice *Who are you?*

Dorothy I – if you please, I am Dorothy, the Small and Meek. We've come to ask you –

LONG SHOT – THRONE

Flame and smoke pouring out.

Oz's Voice (*booming forth and interrupting*) SILENCE!

74

Dorothy (*running back*) Oh! Oh! Jiminy Crickets!

Oz's Voice The Great and Powerful Oz knows *why* you have come! Step forward, *Tin Man*!

Tin Man (*trembling so hard his joints rattle, is shoved forward by Dorothy*) Ohhhh!

Oz's Voice You dare to come to me for a heart – do you? You clinking, clanking, clattering collection of caliginous junk!

Tin Man Ohhh – yes . . . yes, sir – y-y-yes, Your Honor. You see, a while back, we were walking down the Yellow Brick Road, and –

Oz's Voice Quiet!

Tin Man (*running back to the others*) Ohhhh!

Oz's Voice And *you*, Scarecrow, have the effrontery to ask for a brain? You billowing bale of bovine fodder!

Scarecrow (*salaaming before throne*) Y-yes – Yes, Your Honor – I mean, Your Excellency – I – I mean – Your Wizardry!

Oz's Voice Enough!

The Scarecrow returns to his companions.

Oz's Voice Uhhh – and *you*, Lion!

The Lion groans with fear as he is slowly pushed forward.

Oz's Voice *Well?*

CLOSE ON LION

He begins to speak and faints dead away. The others run to him.

Dorothy straightens up from the Lion and turns on the Wizard.

Dorothy (*angrily*) Oh – oh! You ought to be *ashamed* of yourself! Frightening him like that, when he came to you for help!

Oz's Voice *Silence*, whippersnapper!

Dorothy sits down suddenly.

The beneficent Oz has every intention of granting your requests!

CLOSER ON GROUP

The Lion comes out of his faint and sits up.

Dorothy What?

Lion (*full of excitement*) What's that? What'd he say?

Dorothy (*pulling him up*) Oh, come on.

Lion (*getting to his feet*) Huh? What'd he say?

Oz's Voice But first you must prove yourselves worthy by performing a very small task. Bring me the broomstick of the Witch of the West!

Tin Man B-b-b-b-but if we do that, we'd have to kill her to get it!

Oz's Voice Bring me her broomstick and I'll grant your requests! Now go!

Lion But – but what if she kills us first?

Oz's Voice I said *GO!*

LONG SHOT – FOUR

The Lion gives a wailing moan. Camera pans as he turns and runs like mad out of the throne room and into the corridor.

LONG SHOT – CORRIDOR

The Lion comes running forward. Camera pans as he turns and dives through the window with a crash.

FADE OUT

FADE IN ON:
HAUNTED FOREST

Crane truck shot to weird, tremolo music. The Camera pushes downward through a bunch of leafy branches in a very creepy-looking wood. Now it trucks to a signpost:

> HAUNTED FOREST
> WITCHES CASTLE
> 1 MILE

Beneath this is:

> I'D TURN
> BACK IF I
> WERE YOU!

LAP DISSOLVE TO:
LONG SHOT – FOUR

The Scarecrow carries a water pistol and a stick that bends like rubber in the middle. The Tin Man carries a huge wrench, and the Lion carries a fish net and a spray pump with 'Witch Remover' printed on it. They stop and look at signpost.

Lion 'I'd Turn Back If I Were You.'

He nods and deliberately turns around to start back, but the others stop him. He growls as they proceed.

CLOSE SHOT – TWO BLACK OWLS

With illuminated eyes, gazing down from a tree.

MEDIUM SHOT – FOUR

The Lion turns to run, but the Tin Man and Scarecrow at once link their arms firmly in his and turn him back to face the right way, swinging him quickly into the air, however, so that his legs pedal madly in space, all the time crying.

Lion (*bawling*) Oh, look! Look! Oh, look . . .!

CLOSE-UP – TWO CROWS

Blinking their red eyes, in another tree.

Scarecrow I believe there're spooks around here.

Tin Man (*trying to be bold*) That's ridiculous! Spooks! That's silly!

Lion D-don't you believe in spooks?

Tin Man No! Why, on – Oh!

TRICK SHOT

The Tin Man suddenly vanishes straight up.

Dorothy Oh! Oh! Tin Man! Oh! Oh!

He suddenly reappears a few yards farther along the path as he hits the ground with a deafening crash.

Dorothy Oh – oh–

Scarecrow Oh, are you – are you all right?

As the Scarecrow and Dorothy run forward to help him, the Lion remains and repeats to himself in an earnest, anxious voice:

Lion (*trembling with eyes closed*) I do believe in spooks, I do believe in spooks; I do, I do, I do, I do, I do I . . .

MEDIUM SHOT – INT. TOWER ROOM

The Witch watches the image of the Lion in her crystal with Nikko and other winged monkeys.

Lion . . . do believe in spooks; I do believe in spooks; I do, I do, I do, I do, I do, I do! (*Then fades.*)

Witch (*laughing*) You'll believe in more than that before I've finished with you!

Camera pans as she rises and goes to the window, addressing the winged monkeys.

Witch Take your army to the Haunted Forest and bring me that girl and her dog. Do what you like with the others, but I want her alive and unharmed! They'll give you no trouble, I promise you that. I've sent a little insect on ahead to take the fight out of them! Ha, ha, ha, ha, ha, ha! Take special care of those ruby slippers – I want those most of all!

By now the winged monkeys are flying past the window screaming and chattering, so that the Witch has to shout to make herself heard.

Now fly – fly! Fly! Fly! Fly!

Camera pulls back as the Witch stands by the window, silhouetted against the sky with her batlike army passing by.

LAP DISSOLVE TO:
LONG SHOT – SKY

The winged monkeys come flying toward the Camera in flight formation.

MEDIUM SHOT – HAUNTED FOREST

The Four look up in the sky in terror. The winged monkeys swoop down on them.

Two run after Dorothy.

Dorothy Help! Help! Help!

As the Tin Man swings his ax, the monkeys capture him.

Tin Man Go 'way now! Or I'll – I'll . . .

Other monkeys tromp on the Scarecrow.

Scarecrow Help! Help! Oh! Oh!

The two monkeys grab Dorothy.

Dorothy Toto! Toto! Help, Toto!

CLOSE-UP – TOTO

He looks up after Dorothy, barking.

LONG SHOT – HAUNTED FOREST

Dorothy screams as she is carried over the trees.

Another monkey grabs Toto and disappears.

GROUP SHOT AT SCARECROW

He is lying on the ground as the winged monkeys fly off. The Tin Man and Lion come over to help him.

Scarecrow Help! Help! Help!

Tin Man Oh, well, what happened to you?

Scarecrow They tore my legs off and they threw them over there. Then they took my chest out and then they threw it over there –

Tin Man Well – that's you all over.

Lion They sure knocked the stuffin's out of ya, didn't they?

Scarecrow Don't stand there talking! Put me together! We've got to find Dorothy!

Tin Man Now, let's see . . .

LAP DISSOLVE TO:
LONG SHOT – WITCH'S CASTLE

Perched high atop a mountainous rock.

LAP DISSOLVE TO:
CLOSE SHOT – INT. WITCH'S CASTLE
WITCH'S TOWER ROOM

The Witch is talking to Toto in her lap.

Witch (*with diabolical sweetness*) What a nice little dog. (*Puts him in the basket and hands it to Nikko.*) And you, my dear, what an unexpected pleasure. It's so kind of you to visit me in my loneliness.

Dorothy (*in great distress*) What are you going to do with my dog? Give him back to me!

Witch All in good time, my little pretty, all in good time.

Dorothy Oh, please, give me back my dog!

Witch Certainly – certainly. When *you* give *me* those slippers.

Dorothy But the Good Witch of the North told me not to!

Witch Very well! (*savagely to Nikko*) Throw that basket in the river and drown him!

Dorothy (*frantic*) No! No – no! Here – you can *have* your old slippers, but give me back Toto!

Witch (*elated*) That's a good little girl! I knew you'd see reason! (*She stoops down impatiently.*)

81

INSERT (TRICK SHOT) – CLOSE-UP OF WITCH'S HANDS

She grabs at the ruby slippers. They suddenly flash like red fire. The Witch shrieks with pain.

BACK TO SCENE

The Witch shrinks back, staring at her hands and down at the slippers.

Witch Ohhhh! Ohhhh!

Dorothy I'm sorry. I didn't do it.

Witch Oh!

Dorothy Can I still have my dog?

Witch (*savagely*) No! Fool that I am! I should have remembered! Those slippers will never come off . . . as long as you're alive!
(*in a silky voice*) But that's not what's worrying me . . . it's *how* to do it . . . these things must be done delicately, or you hurt the spell . . .

CLOSE SHOT – BASKET

Toto suddenly pushes his head out and scrambles out and across the floor and out the door.

Dorothy Run, Toto, run!

Witch (*furiously to Nikko*) Catch him, you fool!

LONG SHOT – INT. HALLWAY

Toto comes tearing down the steps.

LONG SHOT – EXT. DRAWBRIDGE

Toto comes flying out of the castle just as the drawbridge begins to rise.

CLOSE-UP – TOTO AT THE EDGE OF RISING
DRAWBRIDGE

He hesitates for a moment.

LONG SHOT – DRAWBRIDGE

*As the Winkies rush out of the castle, carrying long
spears, Toto jumps from the bridge and lands among the
rocks on the other side.*

Dorothy Run, Toto, run!

*The Winkies miss Toto when they throw their spears,
and he runs off through the rocks.*

Run, Toto! Run!

CLOSE SHOT – DOROTHY AT WINDOW

Dorothy (*joyfully*) He got away! He got away!

Witch (*savagely*) Ohhhh!

Dorothy turns back from window in fear.

Which is more than you will! Drat you and your dog!
You've been more trouble to me than you're worth, one
way and another, but it'll soon be over now!
(*She seizes a large hourglass off the table and holds it up
and turns it over.*)
You see that? That's how much longer you've got to be
alive.

Dorothy cries.

And it isn't long, my pretty, it isn't long! I can't wait
forever to get those shoes!
(*The Witch goes out of the door and slams and locks it
shut.*)

CLOSE-UP – THE HOURGLASS

With the sand running through.

MEDIUM SHOT – DOROTHY

Camera pans as Dorothy moves over to the throne and sits down by the crystal.

Dorothy (*sobbing*) I'm frightened – I'm frightened, Auntie Em – I'm frightened!

TRICK SHOT – CRYSTAL

Just beside Dorothy begins to swirl and smoke restlessly; and then Aunt Em DISSOLVES IN:

Aunt Em (*calling*) Dorothy . . . Dorothy, where are you? It's me – It's Auntie Em . . . we're trying to find you . . . where are you?

Dorothy (*sobbing*) I'm here in Oz, Auntie Em! I'm locked up in the Witch's castle . . . and I'm trying to get home to you, Auntie Em!

Aunt Em's face has begun to fade from the crystal, having made no sign of hearing Dorothy.

Oh, Auntie Em – don't go away! I'm frightened! Come back! Come back!

The Witch's face suddenly appears in the crystal instead. Dorothy shrinks back from the crystal in terror.

Witch (*mimicking Dorothy*) Auntie Em, Auntie Em! Come back! I'll give you Auntie Em, my pretty! (*She laughs.*)

CLOSE-UP – THE HOURGLASS

With the sand running through.

LAP DISSOLVE TO:
IN A SERIES OF QUICK CUTS

Toto making his way down to the bottom of the rocks and rushing through the forest, barking.

MEDIUM SHOT – CLEARING WHERE DOROTHY
WAS SEIZED

The Tin Man and the Lion are busy stuffing odd strands of straw into the Scarecrow, who lies on the ground. Toto rushes into the clearing, barking furiously.

Tin Man Look! There's Toto! Where'd he come from?

Scarecrow Why, don't you see? He's come to take us to Dorothy!

Tin Man Oh –

Scarecrow Come on, fellas!

Toto barks and leads them down the trail.

LAP DISSOLVE TO:
LONG SHOT – HILLSIDE

Where the Cowardly Lion is fighting his way over the boulders and slippery shale, with the Tin Man holding onto his tail. The Scarecrow is coming up from behind.

The Tin Man slips, hanging onto the Lion's tail to keep from falling.

Lion I – I – I hope my strength holds out.

Tin Man I hope your *tail* holds out! Oh!

LONG SHOT – WITCH'S CASTLE

This shows the great towers of the castle silhouetted against the sky on the peak of the mountain. There is a full moon that makes it almost bright as day.

CLOSE-UP – THE ROCKS

The three appear out of the rocks.

Lion What's that? What's that?

LONG SHOT – THE TOWER OF THE WITCH'S CASTLE

CLOSE SHOT – THE THREE

Scarecrow That's the castle of the Wicked Witch!
Dorothy's in that awful place?

Tin Man Oh, I hate to think of her in there. We've got to
get her out! (*Begins crying.*)

Scarecrow Don't cry now. We haven't got the oil can with
us, and you've been squeaking enough as it is!

Lion Who's them? Who's them?

LONG SHOT – ENTRANCE TO CASTLE

(*As seen by the group*) *guarded by a dozen enormous
Winkie Guards holding wicked-looking weapons.*

Winkies (*chanting as they march*)
O – Ee – Yah! Eoh – Ah!
O – Ee – Yah! Eoh – Ah!
O – Ee – Yah! Eoh – Ah! . . .

CLOSE SHOT – THE ROCKS

Scarecrow I've got a plan how to get in there . . .

Lion Fine. He's got a plan.

Scarecrow . . . and you're gonna lead us.

Lion Yeah – Me?

Scarecrow Yes, you.

Lion I – I – I gotta get her outta there?

Scarecrow That's right.

Lion All right, I'll go in there for Dorothy – Wicked Witch or no Wicked Witch – guards or no guards – I'll tear 'em apart – Woof! I may not come out alive, but I'm goin' in there! There's only one thing I want you fellas to do.

Scarecrow and Tin Man What's that?

Lion Talk me out of it!
(*He starts to turn, but the others stop him.*)

Tin Man No, you don't!

Scarecrow Oh, no!

Lion No? Now wait a minute!

Tin Man Get up here –

They push him forward.

Scarecrow Up!

Lion Now . . .

LAP DISSOLVE TO:
CLOSE-UP – THE HOURGLASS

With the sand running through.

LAP DISSOLVE TO:
MEDIUM SHOT – NEAR ROCK

They watch the Winkie Guards marching. Toto barks. They indicate for him to be silent.

The towering helmets of three huge Winkie Guards rise above them behind the rocks. These are not seen by the group.

They are whispering to each other. By now the Guards have dropped down behind them. The Lion turns and sees them. He tries to speak but cannot. He tries to get their attention, but they shush him.

The Guards pounce on them, and all vanish behind the rocks, from which comes a yelling and a thumping.

Lion Put 'em up!

LAP DISSOLVE TO:
CLOSE-UP – THE ROCKS

The sounds of the fray die down. One by one, three Winkie helmets appear above the rocks. We feel the Winkies have vanquished, if not killed, Dorothy's friends. As they come up from below the rock, the first two are the Tin Man and Scarecrow in the heavy Winkie uniforms, and the third is the Lion with his tail wagging in the air. Toto emerges with a piece of tassel in his teeth.

LONG SHOT – ENTRANCE

The Winkie Guards march up, chanting.

Scarecrow Come on, I've got another idea.

Lion Do – do ya think it'll be polite, droppin' in like this?

Scarecrow and Tin Man Come on . . . come on.

They move through the rocks.

CLOSER ON ENTRANCE

Our three friends march in the picture, then goose-step through the entrance into the castle after the Winkie Guards. The last one is the Lion, who is having a dreadful time with his tail. Toto is bringing up the rear of the procession as the drawbridge is pulled up.

LONG SHOT – INT. CASTLE – ENTRANCE HALL

As they reach across hall, the Winkie Guards turn smartly and march off. Our three duck behind a partition in the wall.

Tin Man Where do we go now?

Lion Yeah!

Toto barks on steps.

Scarecrow (*pointing at Toto*) There!

They run up the stairs after Toto.

LONG SHOT – UPPER HALLWAY

This is outside the door to the Witch's tower room.

Toto barks and then shuffles and scratches at a door.

Scarecrow Wait! We'd better make sure. Dorothy? Are you in there?

Lion It's us!

MEDIUM SHOT – INT. TOWER ROOM

Dorothy (*runs to the door excitedly*) Yes, it's me! She's locked me in!

MEDIUM SHOT – TIN MAN, SCARECROW AND LION

Lion (*excitedly*) Listen, fellas! It's her! We gotta get her out! Open the door!

They discard their spears and uniforms.

LONG SHOT – DOROTHY

Dorothy Oh, hurry! Please, hurry! . . .

CLOSE-UP – THE HOURGLASS

With the sand running through.

Dorothy (*with renewed urgency*) . . . The hourglass is almost empty!

CLOSE SHOT – DOOR

Tin Man (*suddenly*) Stand back!
(*He begins chopping at the door.*)

Dorothy stands back and picks up basket.

CLOSE-UP – THE HOURGLASS

A few grains remain.

IN A SERIES OF QUICK CUTS

The Tin Man breaks in the door with his ax.

Dorothy rushes out and into their arms. The Scarecrow hands her Toto.

Dorothy Oh – oh – oh, Toto! Toto! Oh, Lion darling – I knew you'd come!

Tin Man Dorothy!

Dorothy I knew you would!

Scarecrow Hurry – we've got no time to lose!

They grab Dorothy and run down the corridor.

LONG SHOT – STAIRS

The castle is deserted. Camera pans as they run down the stairs and across the hall toward the entrance doors, which are open wide.

Just as they are reaching the doors, with a deafening crash they slam shut.

MEDIUM SHOT – OF THE FOUR

Beating at the doors and trying to open them. The Tin Man raises his ax to chop. They swing back in terror, as a burst of wild and savage laughter fills the hall.

CLOSE SHOT – WITCH AND NIKKO

Looking down from top of stairs.

Witch Going so soon? I wouldn't hear of it! Why, my little party's just beginning!

MEDIUM SHOT – FOUR

Lion Trapped! Trapped like mice – (*correcting himself*) – er – rats!

LONG SHOT – TOP OF STAIRS

The Witch holds the empty hourglass triumphantly, laughing.

Camera pans down as about thirty or forty Winkies pour into the hall.

CLOSE-UP – TOTO

MEDIUM SHOT – WINKIES

Form in a wide semicircle, surrounding Dorothy and her friends with their spears pointing toward them.

LONG SHOT – SHOOTING DIRECTLY DOWN FROM CEILING

Showing the circle of Winkies closing in on them, step by step.

CLOSE SHOT – WITCH AND NIKKO

Witch (*laughs*) That's right. Don't hurt them right away. We'll let them *think* about it a little first . . . (*Laughs.*)

CLOSE-UP – SCARECROW

He is thinking hard. He looks up at chandelier and sees a rope, which is tied to a hook in the wall.

CLOSE SHOT – WITCH AND NIKKO

At top of the stairs. She screams and flings down the hourglass, which explodes like a bomb in a flash of red smoke.

CLOSE SHOT – FOUR

The Scarecrow suddenly jerks the Tin Man's arm, so the ax comes down and cuts the rope fixed to the wall.

LONG SHOT – SHOOTING DOWN

A huge circular iron candelabrum with flaming candles gives way and falls on the Winkies.

CLOSE SHOT – WITCH

She sees what has happened.

Witch (*shrieking*) Seize them! Seize them! Stop them, you fools! . . .

LONG SHOT – FOUR

The Scarecrow grabs Dorothy's hand and runs through the break in the Winkie line, with the Tin Man and Lion close at his heels.

LONG SHOT – STAIRS

The Witch and Nikko run down the stairs after them.

Witch . . . Stop them! Seize them! Seize them!

LONG SHOT – HALL

The four go rushing into the courtyard, followed by the Winkies.

The four hide on the other side of a pillar and double back in and run through the hall. They run up the stairs.

The Witch follows with the Winkies.

Witch There they go! Ah! Now we've got them! Half you go this way – half you go that way! Hurry! Hurry!

The four reach the top of the stairs.

LONG SHOT – CASTLE FROM ABOVE

Showing the towers, joined by narrow battlements and a wild mountain river flowing past one side. The four come out of the first tower and onto the battlements, and run along it to the second tower.

LONG SHOT – FOUR

They halt in the second tower.

Lion Where do we go now?

Scarecrow This way – Come on!

They run from the second tower.

LONG SHOT – CASTLE FROM ABOVE

They stop at the stairs leading to the tower.

LONG SHOT – WINKIES

Running toward them from the tower.

CLOSE SHOT – FOUR

Dorothy screams.

Scarecrow (*pointing*) Back! Back!

They run the other way back into the tower.

LONG SHOT – BATTLEMENTS OF CASTLE

Winkies enter the tower through both sides.

MEDIUM SHOT – FOUR

They pull up short. Dorothy screams. The Lion groans. They are all terrorized as the Winkies trap them in the tower.

LONG SHOT – INT. TOWER

The Witch enters, followed by Nikko.

Witch (*laughing*) Well! Ring-around-the-rosy! A pocketful of spears! Thought you'd be pretty foxy, didn't cha? Well, the last to go will see the first three go before her . . .

She laughs. The four tremble.

. . . and her mangy little dog, too!

CLOSE SHOT – WITCH

Grins and looks up. Camera pans as she lifts her broom to a burning torch on the wall. The four tremble.

Witch How about a little fire, Scarecrow!

MEDIUM SHOT – FOUR

The Witch thrusts the blazing broom at the Scarecrow. It sets his arm on fire.

Scarecrow (*jumping up and down*) Oh! No! No!

Dorothy screams.

Help! I'm burning! I'm burning! I'm burning! Help! Help! Help! Help!

In defense of the Scarecrow, Dorothy looks around and suddenly sees a bucket of water. She puts Toto down and seizes the bucket.

Witch (*screaming*) Don't touch that water!

Dorothy flings its contents toward the Scarecrow.

CLOSE-UP – WITCH

The water hits her full in the face. It puts out the fire.

LONG SHOT – FOUR, WITCH, ETC.

The Witch screams in agony as she shrinks and shrivels.

Witch Ohhh! You cursed brat! Look what you've done! I'm melting! Melting! Oh, what a world! What a world! Who would have thought a good little girl like you could destroy my beautiful wickedness! Ohhh! Look out! Look out! I'm going! Ohhhh – Ohhhhhhhhhh!

CLOSE ON DOROTHY, TIN MAN, SCARECROW, ETC.

They look down in amazement.

CLOSE-UP – WITCH

She is now no more than her cloak and hat smoldering on the floor.

Toto paws at it. Nikko looks on and claps.

Leader of the Winkies She's – she's dead. You've killed her.

Dorothy I didn't mean to kill her – really I didn't – it's . . . it's just that he was on fire!

Leader Hail to Dorothy! The Wicked Witch is dead!

Winkies (*all drop to their knees before Dorothy*) Hail! Hail to Dorothy! The Wicked Witch is dead!

Dorothy The broom! May we have it?

Leader (*handing it to her*) Please. And take it with you.

Dorothy Oh, thank you so much! Now we can go back to the Wizard and tell him the Wicked Witch is dead!

Winkies The Wicked Witch is dead!

LAP DISSOLVE TO:
LONG SHOT – INT. THRONE ROOM

The atmosphere is the same as the first time they came before Oz.

Dorothy, Scarecrow, Lion and Tin Man are facing the throne. The great head is facing them from the throne.

Oz's Voice (*as shot opens*) Can I believe my eyes? Why have you come back?

Dorothy (*on being handed broomstick by the Scarecrow*) Please, sir, we've done what you told us: we've brought you the broomstick of the Wicked Witch of the West. (*She puts the broomstick down at the foot of the throne.*) We melted her.

Oz's Voice Oh, you liquidated her, eh? Very resourceful.

Dorothy Yes, sir. So we'd like you to keep your promise to us; if you please, sir.

Oz's Voice Not so fast! Not so fast! I'll have to give the matter a little thought! Go away and come back tomorrow!

Dorothy Tomorrow? Oh, but I want to go home *now*!

Tin Man You've had plenty of time already!

Lion (*aggressively*) Yeah!

Oz's Voice (*roaring*) Do not arouse the wrath of the Great and Powerful Oz!

Camera pans as Toto runs to background to curtain hanging around side of throne room.

I said come back tomorrow!

Dorothy If you were really great and powerful, you'd keep your promises!

Oz's Voice Do you presume to criticize the Great Oz?

Toto pulls the curtain aside, and the Wizard is revealed with his back to them talking into a microphone.

You ungrateful creatures!

They stare at the man working the controls of the throne.

Think yourselves lucky that I'm giving you audience tomorrow instead of twenty years from now!
(*A feeling that all is not as it should be makes the man look over his shoulder.*)

Wizard Oh!

Oz's Voice The Great Oz has spoken!

Wizard Oh!
(*He pulls the curtain back.*)

Oz's Voice Pay no attention to that man behind the curtain! The Great Oz has spoken!

Dorothy walks up quietly and pulls the curtain aside.

Dorothy Who are you?

Wizard Who are . . . ah . . . I am the Great and
Powerful . . . Wizard of Oz.

Dorothy (*unable to believe her ears*) You are?

Wizard Uh – yes –

Dorothy I don't believe you!

Wizard No, I'm afraid it's true. There's no other Wizard
except me.

Scarecrow (*indignantly*) You humbug!

Lion and Tin Man Yeah!

Wizard Yes, that's exactly so. I'm a humbug.

Dorothy Oh, you're a very bad man!

Wizard Oh, no, my dear, I – I'm a very good man – I'm just
a very bad wizard.

Scarecrow (*angrily*) What about the heart that you
promised Tin Man?

Wizard Well, I –

Scarecrow And the courage that you promised Cowardly
Lion?

Wizard Well, I –

Tin Man and Lion And Scarecrow's brain?

Wizard (*to Scarecrow*) Why, anybody can have a brain.
That's a very mediocre commodity. Every pusillanimous
creature that crawls on the earth or slinks through slimy
seas has a brain! Back where I come from, we have
universities, seats of great learning – where men go to
become great thinkers – and when they come out, they

think deep thoughts – and with no more brains than you have – *But!* they have one thing you haven't got! A diploma.

(*He picks up several diplomas, selects a parchment scroll with seal and ribbon, and presents it to the Scarecrow.*)

Therefore – by virtue of the authority vested in me by the *Universitatus Committeeatum e pluribus unum*, I hereby confer upon you the honorary degree of Th.D. Heh, heh!

Scarecrow (*terribly impressed*) Th.D.?

Wizard Yeah, that . . . that's Doctor of Thinkology.

Scarecrow (*putting his finger to his head*) The sum of the square roots of any two sides of an isosceles triangle is equal to the square root of the remaining side. Oh, joy, rapture! I've got a brain! How can I ever thank you enough?

Wizard Well, you can't. (*turning to Lion*) As for you, my fine friend, you're a victim of disorganized thinking. You are under the unfortunate delusion that simply because you run away from danger, you have no courage. You're confusing courage with wisdom. Back where I come from, we have men who are called heroes. Once a year they take their fortitude out of mothballs and parade it down the main street of the city. And they have no more courage than you have – *But!* they have one thing that you haven't got! A medal!

(*He takes a big triple-cross medal out of his black bag and pins it on the Lion's skin as he imitates a French Legion general.*)

Therefore, for meritorious conduct, extraordinary valor, conspicuous bravery against wicked witches, I award you the Triple Cross. You are now a member of the Legion of Courage.

(*He kisses Lion on both cheeks.*)

Lion (*overcome*) Hah, hah, shucks, folks, I'm speechless! Hah, hah . . . (*Hides his face.*)

Wizard (*to Tin Man*) As for you, my galvanized friend, you want a heart! You don't know how lucky you are not to have one. Hearts will never be practical until they can be made unbreakable.

Tin Man But I . . . I still want one.

Wizard Back where I come from, there are men who do nothing all day but good deeds. They are called phil . . . er . . . phil . . . er . . . yes . . . er . . . good-deed-doers, and their hearts are no bigger than yours – *But!* they have one thing you haven't got! A testimonial!
(*He takes a huge heart-shaped watch and chain out of his black bag.*)
Therefore, in consideration of your kindness, I take pleasure at this time in presenting you with a small token of our esteem and affection. (*Hands it to Tin Man.*) And remember, my sentimental friend, that a heart is not judged by how much you love, but by how much you are loved by others.

Tin Man (*listening to the watch, in ecstasy, sighs*) Ah, eh, oh, it ticks! (*showing it to Dorothy*)

Dorothy Oh, yes!

Tin Man Listen! Look, it ticks!

Lion (*to Dorothy*) Read . . . read what my medal says! 'Courage!' Ain't it the truth! Ain't it the truth!

Dorothy (*joyfully*) Oh . . . oh, they're all wonderful . . .

Scarecrow (*suddenly – to Wizard*) Hey, what about Dorothy?

Tin Man Yes, how about Dorothy?

Lion Yeah.

Wizard Ah . . .

Lion Dorothy next!

Wizard Yes, Dorothy . . . ah . . .

Dorothy (*sadly*) Oh, I don't think there's anything in that black bag for me.

Wizard Well, you force me into a cataclysmic decision. The only way to get Dorothy back to Kansas is for me to take her there myself.

Dorothy (*her face lighting up*) Oh, will you? Could you? Oh! (*with doubt*) Oh, but are you a clever enough wizard to manage it?

Wizard (*with dignity*) Child, you cut me to the quick! I'm an old Kansas man myself . . . born and bred in the heart of the Western wilderness, premier balloonist par excellence to the Miracle Wonderland Carnival Company – until one day, while performing spectacular feats of stratospheric skill never before attempted by civilized man, an unfortunate phenomena occurred. The balloon failed to return to the fair.

Lion It *did*?

Dorothy Weren't you frightened?

Wizard (*leading them toward the door*) Frightened! You are talking to a man who has laughed in the face of death, sneered at doom, and chuckled at catastrophe. I was petrified! Then suddenly the wind changed, and the balloon floated down into the heart of this noble city, where I was instantly acclaimed Oz, the First Wizard de luxe! (*Laughs*)

Dorothy Oh!

Wizard Times being what they were, I accepted the job, heh, retaining my balloon against the advent of a quick getaway. Ha ha! And in that balloon, my dear Dorothy, you and I will return to the land of *e pluribus unum*! Ha ha! And now . . .

They all laugh and begin walking out of the room, Camera trucking with them.

LAP DISSOLVE:
LONG SHOT – EMERALD CITY SQUARE

On a decorated platform erected in the center of the square and surrounded by the people of Oz stands the gaily striped balloon with Dorothy and the Wizard in it. The Scarecrow, Tin Man and Lion stand near, in charge of the mooring ropes. The balloon reads: STATE FAIR OMAHA. *The square is filled with cheering people.*

Wizard (*as shot opens*) My friends, my friends, I mean *my friends*! . . . This is positively the finest exhibition ever to be shown . . . well . . . eh . . . well . . . be that as it may – I, your Wizard *par ardua ad alta*, am about to embark upon a hazardous and technically unexplainable journey into the outer stratosphere . . .

Crowd cheers.

 . . . to confer, converse, and otherwise hobnob with my brother wizards, and I hereby decree that until what time –
(*aside*)
– if any –
(*aloud*)
– that I return, the Scarecrow by virtue of his highly superior brains, shall rule in my stead, assisted by the Tin Man, by virtue of his magnificent heart, and the Lion, by virtue of his courage! Obey them as you would me! Thank you!

CLOSE-UP – TOTO IN DOROTHY'S ARMS

He suddenly cocks his ears and growls.

CLOSE SHOT – OZ WOMAN WITH CAT IN HER ARMS

The cat meows.

MEDIUM SHOT – DOROTHY IN BALLOON BASKET

Toto jumps out of her arms.

Dorothy Oh, Toto! Come back! Toto! Toto!
(She jumps out of basket.)
Oh, don't go without me! I'll be right with you! Toto!
(She runs down steps.)

LONG SHOT – BALLOON BASKET

Tin Man Stop that dog!

Dorothy Toto!

*The Scarecrow and the Lion drop the ropes to help
Dorothy. The balloon begins to rise.*

Wizard This is a highly irregular procedure! . . . absolutely
unprecedented!

Tin Man Oh, help me! The balloon's going up!

Wizard . . . Ruined my exit!

*Dorothy and the Scarecrow return to the platform as the
balloon rises.*

Dorothy (*in a scream*) Oh! Come back, come back – don't
go without me! Please come back!

Wizard I can't come back! I don't know how it works!
(*waving to the crowd*) Good-bye, folks!

People (*waving back*) Good-bye! Good-bye! Good-bye!
Good-bye!

The balloon passes over the cheering crowd and out of sight.

MEDIUM SHOT – DOROTHY AND TOTO

The Scarecrow, Tin Man and Lion try to comfort her.

Dorothy (*in terrible distress*) Oh, now I'll *never* get home!

Lion Stay with us, then, Dorothy. We all love ya. We don't want ya to go.

Dorothy Oh, that's very kind of you, but this could never be like Kansas. Auntie Em must have stopped wondering what happened to me by now. Oh, Scarecrow, what am I going to do?

Scarecrow (*pointing*) Look! Here's someone who can help you!

LONG SHOT – EMERALD CITY SQUARE

The Witch of the North's bubble floats over the crowd. The people step aside as it comes to rest and fades. Glinda approaches, waving her wand.

People Oh . . . my . . .

Dorothy (*curtsying*) Oh, *will* you help me? *Can* you help me?

Glinda You don't need to be helped any longer. You've always had the power to go back to Kansas.

Dorothy I *have*?

Scarecrow Then why didn't you tell her before?

Glinda Because she wouldn't have believed me. She had to learn it for herself.

Scarecrow and Tin Man look inquiringly at Dorothy.

Tin Man What have you learned, Dorothy?

Dorothy (*thoughtfully*) Well, I . . . I think that it . . . that it wasn't enough just to want to see Uncle Henry and Auntie Em . . . and it's that if I ever go looking for my heart's desire again, I won't look any further than my own backyard; because if it isn't there, I never really lost it to begin with!
(*timidly to* Glinda) Is that right?

Glinda (*nodding and smiling*) That's all it is.

Scarecrow But that's so easy! I should have thought of it *for* you!

Tin Man I should have felt it in my heart!

Glinda No – she had to find it out for herself. Now those magic slippers will take you home in two seconds!

Dorothy Oh! Toto, too?

Glinda Toto, too.

Dorothy (*overjoyed*) Oh, now?

Glinda Whenever you wish.

Dorothy turns delightedly to the others.

Dorothy Oh, dear, that's too wonderful to be true!
(*in a small voice, her eyes in tears*) Oh, it's . . . it's going to be so hard to say good-bye. I love *you* all, too.
Good-bye, Tin Man. Oh, don't cry . . .
(*wiping away his tears, handing him his oil can*)
. . . You'll rust so dreadfully. Here . . . here's your oil can.
(*She kisses him.*)
Good-bye.

Tin Man Now I know I've got a heart . . . 'Cause it's breaking.

Dorothy (*to Lion, kissing him*) Good-bye, Lion. You know, I know it isn't right, but I'm going to miss the way you used to holler for help before you found your courage!

Lion I – I would never've found it if it hadn't been for you.

Dorothy turns to Scarecrow; they look at each other a second, then she puts her arms around him and hugs him.

Dorothy (*whispering in Scarecrow's ear*) I think I'll miss you most of all. (*She kisses him and sobs.*)

Glinda Are you ready now?

Dorothy Yes. Say good-bye, Toto.

She waves Toto's paw at her friends; they wave in return.

Yes, I'm ready now.

Glinda Then close your eyes and tap your heels together three times . . .

CLOSE-UP – RUBY SLIPPERS

Dorothy clicks them together three times.

Glinda . . . and think to yourself, 'There's no place like home; there's no place like home; there's no . . .'

Camera trucks forward to Dorothy as she speaks with her eyes closed.

'. . . there's no place like home; there's no place like home . . .'

Dorothy's face remains in big close-up while superimposed with spiral effect and then close-up of ruby slippers clicking together three times.

'. . . there's no place like home; there's no place like home; there's no place like home . . .'

LONG SHOT – DOROTHY'S HOUSE

Falling toward Camera with a crash to Blackout.

(SEPIA TONE)
FADE IN – CLOSE-UP – DOROTHY – INT.
DOROTHY'S BEDROOM

We are on Dorothy's face, with eyes closed, as she is murmuring:

Dorothy '. . . there's no place like home; there's no place like home; there's no place like home . . .'

A wet cloth is being applied to her forehead.

Aunt Em Wake up, honey.

At this Dorothy opens her eyes and looks up.

Dorothy '. . . there's no place like home; there's no place like home . . . there's no place . . .'

Camera trucks back to see Aunt Em sitting on Dorothy's bed. Uncle Henry is standing, looking down at her anxiously.

Aunt Em Dorothy – Dorothy, dear . . . It's Aunt Em, darling.

Dorothy (*with happy excitement*) Oh, Auntie Em, it's *you* . . .

Aunt Em (*removing the cloth*) Yes, darling.

From offscreen we hear the Professor's voice calling:

Professor Marvel Hello, there! Anybody home? (*He passes by window and stops.*) I . . . I just dropped by

because I heard the little girl got caught in the big –
(*smiling at Dorothy as he sees her*)
Well, she seems all right now.

Uncle Henry Yeah, she got quite a bump on the head. We kinda thought there for a minute she was gonna leave us.

Professor Marvel Oh.

Dorothy But I *did* leave you, Uncle Henry – that's just the trouble! And I tried to get back for days and days –

Aunt Em (*soothingly*) There, there, lie quiet now. You just had a bad dream –

Dorothy No . . .

Hunk, Hickory and Zeke approach the bed.

Hunk Sure – remember me? Your old pal, Hunk?

Dorothy Oh –

Hickory Me, Hickory?

Zeke You couldn't forget my face, could ya?

Dorothy No, but it wasn't a dream. It was a place.
(*She points to the three boys.*)
And you – and you – and you–
(*Points to the Professor.*)
And *you* were there!

Professor Marvel Oh!

Hunk Sure.

They all laugh.

Dorothy (*puzzled*) But you couldn't have been, could you?

Aunt Em (*gently*) Oh, we dream lots of silly things when we –

Dorothy (*with absolute belief*) No, Aunt Em, this was a real truly live place. And I remember that some of it wasn't very nice – but most of it was beautiful! But just the same, all I kept saying to everybody was, 'I want to go home.' And they sent me home!

She waits for a reaction; they all laugh again.

Doesn't anybody believe me?

Uncle Henry (*soberly, softly*) Of course we believe you, Dorothy . . .

Toto crawls on the bed to Dorothy.

Dorothy Oh, but anyway, Toto, we're home – *home*! And this is my room – and you're all here – and I'm not going to leave here ever, ever again, because I love you all! And . . . oh, Auntie Em, there's no place like home!

FADE OUT
FADE IN:

The End

CREDITS

(*Lion roar*)

FADE IN:

Metro-Goldwyn-Mayer
Presents

LAP DISSOLVE TO:

'THE
WIZARD
OF OZ'

Copyright MCMXXXIX in U.S.A.
By Loew's Incorporated
All Rights in the Motion Picture
Reserved Under International Conventions
Passed by the National Board of Review Ars Gratia Artis
A Metro-Goldwyn-Mayer Picture
(Trade Mark)
Produced by
Loew's Incorporated

LAP DISSOLVE TO:

A
VICTOR FLEMING
PRODUCTION

LAP DISSOLVE TO:

with
JUDY GARLAND
FRANK MORGAN
RAY BOLGER
BERT LAHR
JACK HALEY
BILLIE BURKE
MARGARET HAMILTON
CHARLEY GRAPEWIN
AND THE MUNCHKINS

LAP DISSOLVE TO:

Screen Play by
NOEL LANGLEY,
FLORENCE RYERSON,
and EDGAR ALLAN WOOLF

Adaptation by
NOEL LANGLEY

From the Book by
L. FRANK BAUM

LAP DISSOLVE TO:

MUSICAL PROGRAM

Musical Adaptation by
HERBERT STOTHART

Lyrics by   *Music by*
E. Y. HARBURG   HAROLD ARLEN

Associate Conductor GEORGE STOLL

Orchestral and Vocal Arrangements GEORGE BASSMAN

Orchestral and Vocal Arrangements MURRAY CUTTER
(contd.) PAUL MARQUARDT
KEN DARBY

Musical Numbers Staged by BOBBY CONNOLLY

LAP DISSOLVE TO:

Photographed in Technicolor
Photographed in Technicolor by HAROLD ROSSON, A.S.C.
Associate ALLEN DAVEY, A.S.C.
Technicolor Color Director NATALIE KALMUS
Associate HENRI JAFFA

LAP DISSOLVE TO:

Recording Director DOUGLAS SHEARER
Art Director CEDRIC GIBBONS
Associate WILLIAM A. HORNING
Set Decorations EDWIN B. WILLIS
Special Effects ARNOLD GILLESPIE
Costumes by ADRIAN
Character Make-Ups
Created by JACK DAWN
Film Editor BLANCHE SEWELL

Western Electric SOUND SYSTEM
(Trade Mark)

M.P.P.D.A. Seal I.A.T.S.E.
Certificate No. 5364 Insignia

LAP DISSOLVE TO:

Produced by
MERVYN LEROY

LAP DISSOLVE TO:

Directed by
VICTOR FLEMING

CAST

Dorothy	JUDY GARLAND
Professor Marvel	FRANK MORGAN
'Hunk'	RAY BOLGER
'Zeke'	BERT LAHR
'Hickory'	JACK HALEY
Glinda	BILLIE BURKE
Miss Gulch	MARGARET HAMILTON
Uncle Henry	CHARLEY GRAPEWIN
Nikko	PAT WALSHE
Auntie Em	CLARA BLANDICK
Toto	TOTO

The Singer Midgets As The Munchkins